THREE'S A CROWD

"Sorry, I'm not your guy," Clint said, and started to leave the bar.

"Hey, what are ya, yella?" the man called out.

Clint heard the footsteps as the two charged him from behind. He turned, drew his gun, and stuck it into the mouth of the nearest man.

"Right now you got some broken teeth, friend. You want to try for an exploding head?" Clint said. "Want to see your friend's head explode?" he asked the other man.

"Hey, no, we was just havin' fun. . . ."

Clint eased the gun out of the man's mouth, cleaning the barrel on the man's shirt. He flipped a few coins to the bartender. "Drinks for the house," he said, and left.

THE GUNSMITH

212

THE FAMILY FEUD

J. R. ROBERTS

JOVE BOOKS, NEW YORK

FAMILY FEUD

A Jove Book / published by arrangement with
the author

PRINTING HISTORY
Jove edition / September 1999

The Penguin Putnam Inc. World Wide Web site address is
http://www.penguinputnam.com

ISBN: 0-515-12573-3

A JOVE BOOK®
Jove Books are published by The Berkley Publishing Group,
a division of Penguin Putnam Inc.,
375 Hudson Street, New York, New York 10014.
JOVE and the "J" design
are trademarks belonging to Penguin Putnam Inc.

PRINTED IN THE UNITED STATES OF AMERICA

10 9 8 7 6 5 4 3 2 1

ONE

Horses were born to run. At least, that was what Clint Adams believed—especially at times like these, when he was astride Duke and the big gelding was eating up ground with his huge strides.

Of course, he would have liked it better if no one was shooting at him.

He didn't even know who the men were who were shooting at him. He'd been riding along, minding his own business, when suddenly there was a shot, and then another. Before he knew it a group of men—ten? twelve?—were riding at him, firing their weapons. Some were using pistols, not even within range yet, but others were using rifles and soon the air was ripe with lead. He kicked Duke in the side and they took off at a gallop. More than anything he was afraid a stray bullet would strike the big black, since he made such a huge target.

Duke was outdistancing them. He could tell that without even turning around. Still, they weren't giving up. The shots sounded farther away, but they were still shooting at him. Obviously, this was not a group of men who were accustomed to chasing someone. That meant they were not an experienced posse, or an experienced band of outlaws.

Who were they then? And why were they chasing him, trying to kill him?

He thought back to the town he had just left. That seemed the simplest way to go. . . .

Jennings, Arizona, was not a large town. It probably had some things to offer, but if it did they were not readily evident.

However, since Clint wasn't looking for anything beyond some time in a hotel bed, and some rest for Duke, that didn't matter to him.

He rode down the main street, looking for the livery. He decided against asking for directions, as that would draw attention to him. Bad enough he was drawing attention as a stranger; if he started asking questions, he would attract even more. The town livery was usually spitting distance from a town's main street, and by simply keeping his eyes open he eventually found it.

He exchanged pleasantries with the liveryman, who promised to take good care of Duke.

"Biggest damn horse I ever seed," he kept saying.

Clint agreed with him every time.

Once Duke was taken care of, he did what he always did in a new town: He got a room at the hotel and took a stroll around town looking for a likely place for a meal, at the same time admiring what the town had to offer. This one didn't have much, he realized after a while. He finally picked a café and had a meal that was less than memorable. He went to a saloon and had a beer that was not cold. He looked around the place and everything looked worn, including the women. By the time it was dark and he returned to the hotel, he'd decided that Jennings was not a place to spend time. He had, however, ended up with one of the women.

First thing the next morning, though, he showed up at the livery, collected Duke, and rode out of town. The next thing he knew, men were shooting at him, and he had no idea why. . . .

And they still were—chasing and shooting and not giving up, even though they were falling further behind.

Clint wondered what they'd do, if they were truly inexperienced, if he turned Duke and started riding toward them, firing his gun. He knew he could take a few of them before they knew what was happening, but he'd be risking a stray bullet striking either him or Duke. He could also down a few of their horses, but he didn't relish doing that. Why kill a horse because the man on his back was being foolish?

So he rode on, figuring that sooner or later he would outdistance them and they'd have to give up—give up, or track him.

What were the chances there was an experienced tracker among them?

Still, if he outran them and left them behind he'd always wonder why they were chasing him. Had they recognized him from far off? Did all of them think that if they gunned him down they'd all be famous? Usually when somebody wanted to kill him and use that score to build up his own reputation, it was one man wanting to face him head-on. This was different.

Maybe someone in town thought he had a price on his head. *He* knew for sure that there had never been a poster out on him, but maybe they didn't know that.

He looked behind him and saw that he and Duke had put a comfortable distance between themselves and their pursuers. The men had stopped firing their weapons, but they were still coming.

Clint slowed Duke's progress just a mite, giving him sort of a moving breather, and then thought back again to his stay in Jennings, but he ran it through his mind slower this time.

TWO

He'd ridden down the main street, attracting some attention but not a lot. He tried to remember if he'd met anyone's eyes, or if anyone looked as if they'd recognized him. He didn't think either was the case. People saw a man on a horse, realized he was a stranger, but they didn't really pay him very close attention.

The liveryman, he'd been much too interested in Duke to pay him any mind at all. He doubted very much the man knew who he was. He was, however, the first person in town he'd exchanged words with, but they were congenial words. On top of that, the man was too old to be galloping a horse, firing a gun at the same time.

Not the liveryman.

He'd spoken with the desk clerk at the hotel, a young man who had smiled and welcomed him to Jennings. The young man asked him how long he was going to stay, to which Clint replied he wasn't sure. "Let's start with one night and work on it from there," he'd suggested.

Certainly, the clerk had not been offended. He'd simply handed Clint his key and said, "That's fine, sir."

After that, he didn't see the clerk again. There was an-

other man behind the desk when he returned, but they had
never spoken.

So, neither of the desk clerks seemed likely to be involved.

Of course, he hadn't returned to the hotel alone, but that
came later. . . .

He'd walked around town, just strolling and taking a look.
He might have met the eyes of a person or two, exchanged
a look with a woman or two, but he hadn't spoken to anyone until he picked out the café.

A waiter had seated him, taken his order, and served him.
There were other diners who had paid him no mind, but
had kept the waiter busy enough that they hadn't had much
of a conversation beyond what he was going to eat.

When the food came he had tasted it and found it wanting, but he hadn't commented to the waiter about it, and
he didn't think he'd made any kind of face. After he finished eating, he paid the bill and left. Not a cross word or
a sideways glance.

Not the waiter, or the cook.

After that he found a saloon called The Golden Branch. He
went inside, ordered a beer, and found it lukewarm. It was
wet, though, so he hadn't complained.

Beer in hand, he had looked the place over. The tables
and chairs were worn, the gaming tables well used. He
remembered that three saloon girls had approached him,
making offers with their eyes and mouths. He had talked
to all three but didn't make any offers, and they soon tired
of him and went off to find a more likely customer. None
of them seemed to take it to heart, though. There were
plenty of men in the place.

And then he saw the fourth girl. Not as old as the others,
or as worn-looking. In fact, she walked around the room
looking worried, as if she was afraid someone *would* make
some kind of an offer . . . and then she saw him.

When she got closer he saw that she was about twenty-four, dark haired and pretty, with pale skin and small, firm breasts.

"Hello," she said.

"Hi."

"Would you buy me a drink, please?"

"Sure," he said. He waved at the bartender, who brought her a beer.

"Why me?" he asked. "I see a lot of men in here who would be glad to buy you a drink."

She sipped the beer, made a face as she found it luke-warm.

"They'd want something else, too."

"Is that part of your job?"

"It's not supposed to be," she said, "but the other girls . . ."

"Is this your first night?" he asked.

She shook her head, then said, "First week, fourth night."

"And the other girls say you have to sleep with some of the men?"

"They say it's the only way to make money."

"What's your boss say about it?"

"He says it's up to me."

"He doesn't want a cut?"

"No," she said, "he just wants me to do my job while I'm here. What I do after work is my business."

"What's your name?"

"Laurie."

"Sounds like no one is putting any pressure on you, Laurie."

"Well, no . . ."

"Except maybe yourself."

She held her beer mug in both hands, but didn't drink from it again.

"You don't have to drink beer, you know."

"I can't drink whiskey."

"Just have the bartender give you a sarsaparilla when someone buys you a drink," he suggested. "Nobody will ask what it is."

"That's smart," she said. "Thanks."

"Is there another problem?" he asked. "One you're not telling me?"

She hesitated, then said, "You look kind."

"Thank you," Clint replied. "I hope I am."

"Can I come back to your room tonight?"

"Why?"

"Well . . ."

"Would that make you feel safe the rest of the night?" he asked. "To be able to tell men that you're already spoken for?"

"Yes."

"Fine," he said. "You go ahead and tell them you're with me."

She smiled for time first time and it made her look even younger. "Thanks."

"Don't mention it."

"I'll see you later, then."

"All right."

She put the beer on the bar and went off into the crowd, as if she were suddenly wearing a suit of armor.

"Can I get a fresh beer?" he asked the bartender.

THREE

Maybe that was it.

Riding along, maintaining the distance between him and his pursuers, Clint wondered if it was the girl. Did she have a boyfriend, or a husband, with enough influence to get a dozen other men to chase him down?

Clint waited around the saloon for Laurie to finish working. He nursed a couple more lukewarm beers and watched men gamble and lose. He noticed that there was no private poker game going on; all of the games—blackjack, faro, roulette—were house-run games, with the odds firmly on the side of the house.

Finally, Laurie approached him as the gaming tables were being covered and the bartender was announcing last call for drinks.

"I'm finished," she said.

"Where's your room?" he asked.

"Upstairs," she said, "but I don't want to go there."

"Why not?"

"I . . . don't feel safe."

"Is someone bothering you?"

She hesitated, then repeated, "I just don't feel safe."

9

"You don't even know who I am," he said. "You don't know my name."

"You'll tell me," she said.

"It's Clint."

"Can we go to your hotel, Clint?" she asked. "I'm really tired."

Clint wondered what she expected from him, or what she thought he expected from her. He knew what any other man would expect.

"All right," he said, "let's go."

When they walked through the lobby of the hotel, the desk clerk was dozing. He never saw a thing. Clint was sure of that.

They got up to his room and he turned the lamp up. She moved to the bed and then, suddenly, dropped her dress to the floor. She turned to face him, totally naked.

He caught his breath. Her body was beautiful, with small, firm breasts tipped with dark brown nipples, and not an ounce of fat on her, anywhere.

"How do you want me?" she asked.

He hesitated, knowing that any man would have taken her there and then. He felt his body reacting to her, but he'd never paid for sex in his life, and he did not expect it as payment, itself—especially not for kindness.

He walked to his saddlebags and took out an extra shirt.

"I want you in that," he said, tossing it to her.

She caught it, looking confused.

"I don't understand," she said. "I thought—"

"You asked me for a kindness, Laurie," he said. "Didn't you?"

"Yes, but—"

"I don't charge for kindnesses," he said. "Not money, and not sex. If you want to have sex with me, that's one thing. If you're using it to pay a price, I'm not interested. You can put that shirt on, get in bed, and go to sleep."

"Where will you sleep?"

"Right next to you, and I won't touch you."

She put the shirt on thoughtfully, buttoning it carefully. She picked up her dress and draped it over a chair, then pulled the sheets back and got into bed.

Clint stripped down to his underwear, washed up using the basin and pitcher on the dresser, turned down the lamp on the wall, and then got into bed next to her.

They lay there quietly for a few moments and then she asked, "Would it be too much to ask you to hold me?"

"No," he said, "not too much, at all."

He lifted his arm and she scooted over next to him, putting her head on his shoulder. Their bare legs touched, their hips, and he could feel her heat through the shirt. He had an erection, but unless she indicated that she wanted to have sex he wasn't going to do anything but hold her until she fell asleep.

He waited to see if she'd make a move, perhaps slide her hand down his leg, into his underwear. He admitted he was hoping for that, but in the end she simply fell asleep on his shoulder—the left one, leaving his right arm free to grab for the gun on the bedpost if need be. She fell asleep, and then he did shortly after.

Nothing happened . . . then. . . .

He woke during the night and felt Laurie lying against him. He thought it was an accident, that she'd simply moved during the night, but then her hand landed on his hip, then his thigh, then moved around and slipped into his underwear. By the time she grasped him he was hard.

"Roll onto your back," she whispered.

"Laurie," he said, "you don't have to—"

"Shhh," she said, kissing his bare back, "I want to . . ."

He dutifully rolled onto his back. He had to lift his hips to help her remove his underwear, and then her mouth was on him, all over him. She kissed his belly, his thighs, slid her hands beneath his balls to cup them. She ran her lips up and down the length of him, and then her tongue. Finally, she opened her mouth and took him inside. She began to ride him wetly with her mouth, up and down, sucking him avidly while she caressed his balls with one hand and let her other hand simply roam. Finally, both her hands were cupping his buttocks as she continued to suck him until he couldn't take any more and exploded into her mouth. . . .

Later, he woke her by lying behind her spoon fashion and stroking her between her legs with his fingers. When she was awake and wet, he slid down between her legs and returned the favor to her. He eagerly licked and kissed her wetness, lapping it up, until he had her worked into a frenzy. She grabbed him by the hair suddenly, not to pull him away but to keep him there, and then she was bucking like an unbroke filly as waves of pleasure ran over her.

Clint didn't stop there, though. Before she could recover he moved atop her and slid into her, burying the entire length of himself in her steamy depths. They moved together that way for a very long time, it seemed, until he groaned out loud and exploded again just seconds before she also cried out and scraped his back with her nails, hammered his bare buttocks with the heels of her feet. . . .

He woke in the morning before she did, dressed quietly, and left the room. He still wasn't sure what had happened. Earlier in the evening she'd seemed one kind of girl, one not suited to her job, but then in bed she'd changed dramatically. Rather than try to figure it out, though, or wake her to talk about it, he went to the livery, having decided that he wouldn't spend any more time in Jennings, Arizona.

He rode out of town and it was only a matter of hours before he heard the first shots, saw the men riding down on him with bad intentions.

Maybe she was angry that he hadn't said good-bye?

Yeah, right, and she'd sent twelve armed men after him to tell him that.

Not Laurie.

He was riding hell-for-leather, in danger of pushing Duke to the limit—or beyond. And he still didn't know why. . . .

FOUR

Clint reined Duke in as he topped a rise and turned to look behind him. He'd well-outdistanced the riders, but they were still coming. The ideal thing would have been for them to stop and talk to him, but the fact that they'd begun firing at him without warning ruled that out. His next best bet was to talk to someone else about it. That meant making it to the next town and talking to the sheriff there. Maybe with a badge-toter on his side he could find out what was going on.

He rode down the other side of the rise. He didn't know what the next town would be, but he had to stop there and look for help. His only other alternative would lead to bloodshed, and since he didn't know who these men were—outlaws or lawmen—he didn't want to start shooting.

Not yet.

The next town turned out to be a place called Perryville, and it was even smaller than Jennings had been. Clint could tell that Perryville did not have a telegraph office: There were no wires leading into town. It had to have a lawman, though. Most towns did.

Clint figured he had a half hour at most before the men chasing him came riding into town. Much as he would have liked a drink, instead he rode directly to the sheriff's office, which he found in the center of town. He dismounted, grateful at least for the chance to give Duke a rest.

He walked to the door of the office and tried it, found it locked. He knocked, but there was no answer. There was a window, but it was so covered with grime that he couldn't see inside. That was a bad sign. The sheriff could have been the type who didn't care about windows, but it was more likely that the dirt had built up on the window over time. That meant there was no law in Perryville.

There wasn't much foot traffic in Perryville, either, he found as he turned away from the window and looked for somebody to ask. Seemed like he was going to have to go to the saloon after all.

He'd passed one on the way in, so he grabbed Duke's reins and walked the big gelding over. As he had done in front of the sheriff's office, he grounded the reins instead of tying the animal off. He knew Duke wasn't going anywhere.

Clint knew he was in trouble when he entered the saloon. It was midday and the bartender was alone except for one man sitting at a table.

Ghost town, Clint thought, *or damn close to it.*

"You lost?" the bartender asked. Further proof that he was not going to find what he was seeking here.

"I was looking for the sheriff," Clint said.

"Keep looking," the bartender said. "Ain't had one in a month of Sundays. Beer?"

"Is it cold?"

"Sure."

Clint doubted it, but took one. To his surprise, it *was* cold.

"You musta come from Jennings," the bartender said.

"Why do you say that?"

"They serve warm beer."

"Wish I'd know that before," Clint said. "I never would have stopped there."

"Cold beer's about all we got in this town," the man said.

"How many people here?"

"I've lost count," the bartender said. "Five. Maybe six."

"What happened?"

The man shrugged.

"People just up and left."

"What about you?"

"Probably will, in a few weeks, or months. I'll probably be the last to leave."

"What about him?" Clint asked, indicating the man seated at the table. Since Clint's arrival the man had put his arms on the table and laid his head down on them.

"He'll be next to last."

"Who is he?"

"That's our mayor."

FIVE

Clint left Perryville without looking over his shoulder. If they were following his tracks at all they'd ride into town and take some time to find out if he was there. By then he'd be well on his way to the next town, which, according to the bartender, was called Bridesmaid.

"Don't look at me that way," the bartender said, quickly. "That's what it's called."

"Why?"

"You can find that out when you get there," the man said.

The bartender also told Clint that they had a lawman, and a telegraph key.

"In Bridesmaid?" Clint asked.

"It's a fair-sized town."

As he left Perryville he knew he had about fifty miles to go to get to Bridesmaid—a day's ride on a normal horse. He could make it quicker on Duke, but he expected to have to camp before he got there, because it was late now. He figured to ride in at midday tomorrow.

He knew he'd be taking a risk making camp, even a cold camp, but he felt his inexperienced pursuers probably wouldn't find him.

In fact, he was starting to feel pretty certain that he could lose them completely if he wanted to—but then he'd never find out why they were after him in the first place, and that would nag at him for a long time.

"Just a few more hours, big boy," he said to Duke, patting his big neck, "and then we'll take a long break."

One that he'd need, probably even more than Duke would.

Clint hated cold camps. That was because he loved coffee, which was the first thing you gave up when you made a cold camp. Second, he didn't like beef jerky much, and that was virtually all you could eat in a cold camp, unless you had some canned goods, which he didn't. After all, he had no idea when he'd left Jennings that he'd be *making* a cold camp anytime soon.

He chewed on his jerky and kept alert for any sounds. Later, he lay down and pulled his blanket over him, secure in the belief that Duke would sound the alarm if anyone approached the camp. He removed his gun belt and laid it right near his head, where he could reach it quickly.

He woke in the morning with Duke nudging him with his nose. It wasn't an alarm, just a wake-up call.

"All right, all right," he said grumpily, rolling out of his blanket. "I'm up."

He longed for a cup of coffee so he saddled Duke immediately and set off for Bridesmaid. He was almost as curious to find out who would give a town a name like that—and why—as he was to find out who was shooting at him.

He rode into Bridesmaid at midday. The town had much more in common with Jennings than it did with Perryville. This town, however, showed signs of progress. There were new buildings, still smelling of the newly cut wood they had been built with, and some newly opened streets branching off from the main thoroughfare. Also, the street was covered with people going on about their daily business, on foot, on horseback, or by wagon.

Once again he found the livery on his own rather than asking for directions. In truth, the street might have been busy enough to cover his arrival, so that no one realized there was a stranger in town.

He had decided to make his stand here. Even if the twelve men rode into town later the same day he doubted they'd start shooting up the street, and by that time he would have spoken with the sheriff and filled him in on the problem.

So he put Duke up in the livery, got himself a hotel room, and then walked over to the sheriff's office.

It would be nice to get things back to normal.

SIX

The sheriff's name was Wills—it was on a shingle hanging outside the office: SHERIFF P. WILLS—and he was in his office when Clint entered. He noticed that the office windows were spotless.

"Can I help you?" the man asked.

He was in his thirties, tall and well-built with a well-cared-for mustache and black as night hair that was cut short. A pleasant-looking man with a gun that looked new. Clint wondered if that was from not being used, or if it was simply new, replacing one that had gotten worn out. He was willing to bet on the former. The sheriff didn't have the look.

"I seem to have a problem, Sheriff, and I need a man with a badge to clear it up."

"Is that so?" Wills asked. "Something that happened in town?"

"No," Clint said, "I only just arrived."

"Well, then, you saved me the trouble of coming to see you," the lawman said. "I usually interview all the town newcomers. Much obliged."

"Well, you may not thank me when you hear the problem I've brought you."

The man leaned back in his chair and said, "Why don't

23

you tell me about it and I'll see if I can help.''

Clint told it to him as briefly as possible, that he was being chased by nearly a dozen men who were intent on shooting him on sight.

''And you don't know these men?'' the sheriff asked, when he was finished.

''I actually don't know,'' Clint said. ''I haven't let them get close enough to get a good look at any of them.''

''Might pay to have a talk with them, don't you think?'' the man asked.

''Yes, but there was too much lead flying at the time. That's what I'm hoping you can help me do, talk to them.''

''Are they coming here?'' The sheriff seemed alarmed by the prospect.

''I'm sure they are, if they're trailing me,'' Clint said.

''But . . . we can't have any trouble here,'' Wills said. ''This is a quiet town, a busy town. Shooting on the streets . . . somebody could get hurt.''

''Yes,'' Clint said, ''me, if you don't help me find out who these men are and why they want to kill me.''

''Why don't you talk to the sheriff in Jennings?'' Wills asked.

''I can't go back to Jennings,'' Clint said. ''That's got to be where these men are from.''

''Why can't they be from someplace else?'' Wills asked. ''Maybe they followed you to Jennings.''

Clint stared at the man for a few moments in disbelief. Why hadn't he thought of that? Why did he think that whatever had happened *had* happened in Jennings?

''You have a point there, Sheriff.''

''So maybe you need to go back *past* Jennings, to wherever you were before that.''

''Maybe I do,'' Clint said, ''but maybe we can stop the whole thing right here, in Bridesmaid—who named this town, anyway?''

''Can't say as I know, actually,'' Wills replied. ''I never asked. What's wrong with the name?''

"Nothing, I guess," Clint said—only he didn't think he'd ever want to tell someone that *he* was the sheriff of Bridesmaid.

"Will you help me?"

"Mister—I'm sorry, what's your name?"

That was the only part of the story Clint had held back up to now. It was time to see the sheriff's reaction to his name.

"It's Adams, Sheriff," he said, "Clint Adams."

"Well, Mr. Adams, I don't think it's my jurisd—Adams?" The man stopped short.

"That's right."

"*Clint* Adams?"

"That's what I said."

"But . . . but no, we *can't* have you here," Wills stammered. "That would just cause *so* much trouble. These men, *they* must know who you are—"

"One would think so, or else why would they be shooting at me?"

"Mr. Adams, uh, you have to leave town right away, before they get here."

"I'm safer here than I am on the open trail, Sheriff," Clint said. "Don't you think?"

"My *town* isn't safer with you here," Wills said. "You *have* to leave."

"You won't help me?"

"You're the—the G-Gunsmith!" Wills stuttered. "Why would you need my help?"

"Because I need a lawman."

"But you could just . . . defend yourself . . ."

"Against twelve angry men?"

"B-but, your reputation . . . twelve men shouldn't be a prob—"

"You think I can stand up to twelve men?" Clint asked incredulously.

"Mr. Adams," the sheriff said, trying to calm himself, "I don't know how many men you can stand up to or not;

I only know that you cannot stand up to them *here*. Not in Bridesmaid.''

"Believe me, Sheriff," Clint said, "if I didn't have to be in a town called Bridesmaid I wouldn't be. Look, if you're afraid, all you have to do is stand with me. They won't shoot if they see the badge."

"A-afraid?" Wills asked. "I didn't say I was afraid. I just don't want my people being hurt."

"Then come outside the town with me. We'll wait for them there."

"What makes you think they won't just shoot both of us on sight?"

"If you tell them I'm in your custody, they'll talk," Clint said—at least, he hoped they would.

"Look, Mr. Adams, I sympathize. I wouldn't want twelve men after me, but I can't help you. This is not Bridesmaid business, and you are not a citizen of Bridesmaid."

"I'm a guest in your town," Clint pointed out.

"Yes, and I don't want to be rude, b-but I would like you to leave."

"Or what?" Clint asked. "Are you going to put me in a cell?"

The sheriff smiled nervously.

"Let's be realistic, Mr. Adams. I don't think I could put you into a cell if you didn't want me to. Why don't you just leave?"

For a moment Clint was tempted to push the lawman and see what he was made of, but in the end he decided it wasn't worth it.

"Fine," Clint said. "I'll leave. I'll find help somewhere else. What could I expect of the sheriff of a town called Bridesmaid?"

He turned to leave, but when he got to the door he heard a familiar sound—the sound of a handgun being cocked—a spanking new handgun.

"I'll ask you to put your hands in the air, Mr. Adams," Wills said, "or I'll have to shoot you."

SEVEN

"In the back?" Clint asked.

No answer.

"Are you that afraid of me, Sheriff?"

Still no answer.

"What's this about, Sheriff?" Clint asked. "You wanted me out of your town, I was leaving. You don't have to do this."

"I can't let you leave."

"That's quite change of heart you've had there, Sheriff," Clint said. "Why can't you let me leave?"

"Because of what happened."

Clint frowned. Did he mean in Jennings?

"What happened?"

"Like you don't know," the sheriff said. "That phony story about not knowing why those men are chasing you. What did you hope to accomplish with that?"

"It's the truth."

"I got a telegram telling me what happened in Jennings," Wills said, "telling me what I should do if you showed up here."

"And what was that? To shoot me in the back?"

"To hold you until the posse gets here."

"So that's what they are? A posse?" Clint asked.

"They're a pretty poor excuse for a posse, if you ask me."

"I didn't," Wills said. "I'm gonna have to ask you for your gun, Adams."

"You can ask me for it, friend," Clint said, "but I'm not about to give it to you."

"I have a gun on you."

"I know you do," Clint said, "but if you want my gun, you're going to have to walk over here and take it yourself."

No reply.

"See, I don't think you have the guts to do that, Sheriff, so you sure as hell don't have the guts to shoot me. In fact, you haven't got the guts for this job, and you know it. That's why you're so nervous."

Wills wiped some sweat from his face with the sleeve of his free arm and asked, "How do you know I'm nervous?"

"You're sweating, my friend," Clint said. "I can smell you from here."

Wills knew he was right. Even he could smell the sharp stench of his fear, and it sickened him. Clint Adams was right, he wasn't right for this job. He'd always been afraid something like this was going to happen, something where he'd have to act like a real lawman, and now it had.

"If I was to let you hold me, Sheriff, and turn me over to them, do you know what would happen?"

"What?"

"They'd lynch me in the street."

"They wouldn't dare."

"Why? Because you'd stop them? I don't think so. If you turn me over to them you're killing me, as sure as if you pulled the trigger yourself—and that's the only way you're going to stop me from leaving right now, by pulling the trigger."

"Adams—"

"I'm going out the door," Clint said. "Don't make me kill you."

"Don't make me, Adams—"

"I can't make you do something you're not capable of doing, son," Clint said. "Good-bye."

Clint opened the door, stepped outside, and closed it, then released the breath he was holding. He figured he was either going to get shot in the back, or he'd have to kill the lawman, and he didn't want either to happen.

He hurried to the livery and saddled Duke up, apologizing to the big black gelding for not giving him the rest he deserved.

"Neither one of us is getting any rest, big fella," he said, mounting up. "Not in Bridesmaid."

He never did find out about the town's name.

EIGHT

When he made camp that night, he fixed some coffee, but still only had beef jerky to eat. He hadn't had time to outfit himself at all, yet.

He still didn't know if the men were chasing him for something that had happened in Jennings. He hadn't even gotten that much from the young sheriff.

Over coffee and jerky he tried to replay some of the places he visited before Jennings. He'd ridden into Arizona from New Mexico, where he had stopped at the ranch of a friend, Toby Carmichael. . . .

The standing invitation for Clint to come and stay at the Carmichael spread had been standing for quite a long time. Clint thought it was time to take his friend up on the offer.

The spread was impressive. Corrals seemed to spread out for miles, and the only thing bigger than the barn was the huge house. Clint was amazed at how well Toby was doing; but then, he'd always been a smart man. He had found ways to make money on not only cattle and horses, but timber, as well.

The nearest town to the spread was Haywood. As Clint rode through, he realized that it was right in the midst of expanding. He wondered how much his friend's success reflected in the town's success.

He passed through the town on his way to Carmichael's ranch. Never exchanged a word with anyone. In fact, he didn't speak to anyone until he reined in Duke in front of Carmichael's house.

"Help ya?" a man wearing dusty work clothes asked.

"I'm looking for Toby."

"Who's lookin'?"

"Clint Adams."

The man, whose gaze to that point could only be called lazy, sharpened his look.

"The Gunsmith?"

"Just tell him Clint's here."

"Wait a minute."

While the man went into the house, Clint dismounted and looked over at one of the corrals, where a man was trying to break a horse. That would explain why the man he'd spoken with was all dusty and dirty.

"Come on in, Mister," the man said from the door.

Clint dropped Duke's reins to the ground and approached the door.

"Ain'tcha gonna tie your horse?"

"He's not going anywhere," Clint said.

As Clint stepped inside he saw Toby Carmichael coming toward him with his hand outstretched. He was shocked, because his friend seemed to have put on a hundred pounds in the seven or eight years since he'd seen him last.

"Clint, by God," Carmichael said, grabbing his hand and pumping it. "It's damn good to see you." Carmichael's hand was big and well-padded, but work-hardened nonetheless.

"Thought I'd finally take you up on your offer," Clint said, "if it still stands."

"It stands just where it's been for the past eight years. Clint, this is my foreman, Jake Wade."

Clint turned toward the man and they shook hands.

"Sorry about the dirt," Wade said, withdrawing his hand. "Breakin' broncs is dirty work."

"No problem," Clint said, resisting the urge to wipe his hand on his pants leg.

"Well, I better get back to it," Wade said. "Good to meet you."

"You, too."

Wade left, and Carmichael took Clint by the arm and pulled him along.

"You look like you could use a drink."

"Just to cut the dust," Clint said.

Carmichael led him to a well-furnished room and poured him a brandy from a crystal decanter. The glass was also crystal.

"Very fancy," Clint commented.

"It's good stuff, too," Carmichael said. "Betty makes me buy it."

"How is Betty?"

"Great, she's great," Carmichael said, but his tone of voice was false. Clint had the feeling something was very wrong.

"Where is she?"

"She's . . . not here right now."

"Has she gone away?"

"Well . . . not exactly . . ." Carmichael sat down behind his desk, his brandy forgotten in his hand.

"Toby?"

Carmichael stared at Clint for a few moments, then said, "Hell, yes, something's wrong, Clint."

"What is it?"

"Harry Sheets."

"Who's Harry Sheets?"

"He owns the spread next to mine. It's almost as big, and gettin' bigger. He's trying to ruin me."

"How long has this been going on?"

"Years. At least five or six, since he first came here. He had lots of money behind him, started buying up land. He used a loophole to grab some prime timberland of mine. He's been eating away at me for years.''

''What's that got to do with Betty?''

Carmichael put his brandy glass down on his desk.

''She left me.''

''What?''

''Well, look at me,'' Carmichael said. ''Look how fat I've gotten. Betty stayed beautiful, even as she got older. Forty-five years old, Clint, and she's more beautiful than ever.''

''What's that got to do with Harry Sheets?''

Carmichael hesitated, then reached down, opened a drawer, and took out a bottle of whiskey. He dumped his brandy out and poured the crystal tumbler full of whiskey, then held the bottle out to Clint.

''That brandy shit's good for nothing. Want some of this instead?''

''Sure.''

Clint looked around for someplace to put the brandy.

''Just pour it out on the damn floor. I'll have it cleaned up.''

Clint hesitated, then shrugged and did it. He held the glass out and Carmichael filled it with whiskey.

They both drank half of it down, shuddered, and looked at each other.

''You want to tell me what all this has got to do with Betty leaving you?''

''Sheets,'' Carmichael said.

''You said that,'' Clint replied. ''What's he got to do—''

''That's where she went,'' Carmichael said. ''She left me and went to Harry Sheets.''

NINE

"It was partly my fault," Carmichael explained. "I got all caught up in building my empire, I let myself go, started eating well and drinking well . . . look at me. You must have been shocked when you saw me."

"I was," Clint said bluntly. He didn't think his friend needed coddling at this point.

"You hid it real well."

"Toby, why don't you go and get her back?"

"On one hand I want to do that," he said, "and on the other hand I don't want the slut back."

"What's this Sheets like?"

"He's young, about forty—younger than us, anyway—and very rich. I mean, he was rich when he came here from the East. It's taken me a long time to build up what I have, Clint, but he *came* here rich and started *buying* what he wanted. Now, he buys Betty whatever she wants."

"Don't you think he'll get tired of her?"

"Who could get tired of a woman as beautiful as Betty?" Carmichael asked.

"Apparently, you did," Clint said.

Carmichael insisted that Clint stay at the house and showed him to a guest room. Once he knew where it was, Clint

35

went out to take care of Duke. He walked the big gelding
to the barn, found an empty stall, then unsaddled him and
brushed him down. While he was giving Duke some feed
someone entered the barn. Clint came out of the stall and
saw the foreman, Jake Wade, standing there.

"Can we talk?" Wade asked.

"Sure," Clint said. "Here, or somewhere else?"

"Here's good," Wade said.

"What about?"

"The boss."

Clint remained silent.

"He needs help, Adams. A lot of it."

"What kind of help?"

"Did he tell you about Sheets?"

"Yes." Clint answered carefully, because he wasn't sure
what the foreman knew.

"And did he tell you about Mrs. Carmichael?"

"What about her?"

"That she left him for Sheets?"

Apparently, the foreman knew everything.

"Yes, he told me."

"He talks about you all the time, Adams," Wade said.

"Then I think you better call me Clint."

"Clint," Wade said, "you got to do something."

"Like what?"

"Like get Mrs. Carmichael back."

"How can I do that, Jake?"

"Talk to her," Wade said, "tell her how much the boss
loves her."

"Why would she listen to me?"

"She's gotta listen to somebody," Wade said. "She's
gotta come back. Without her the boss ain't gonna put up
a fight anymore. Harry Sheets is gonna roll right over us.
The boss might even sell out to him."

"Toby wouldn't do that," Clint said. "It's taken him a
long time to build all of this up. He's not just going to give
it up."

"He ain't got no fight in him no more, Clint," Wade said. "You watch him, and listen to him. You'll see."

"I tell you what," Clint said. "I will watch and listen, and if I think there's something I can do to help, I will. Is that good enough?"

"It'll have to be for now, I guess," Wade said. "Thanks for listenin'. I got to get back to work."

Clint watched the man leave the barn, his shoulders slumped. He seemed pretty defeated himself. Clint knew Toby Carmichael was down, but down enough to give it all up? He was going to have to look and listen real well for the next couple of days.

TEN

Clint watched and listened to his friend for two days, and at the end of that time he was convinced that the foreman was right. There was no fight left in Toby Carmichael. Clint sought out Wade and found him by the corrals, watching his men work with some of the horses.

"I think you're right," he said.

"So what are you gonna do?"

"I'll go and talk to Betty Carmichael. I'll need directions to the Sheets place."

"Don't go today," Wade said. "Go tomorrow."

"Why?"

"Tomorrow's the day Sheets goes into town himself to conduct business. Mrs. Carmichael will be at the house."

"Okay," Clint said, "I'll go tomorrow."

However, being in the house with Carmichael was so depressing that Clint spent the rest of the day watching the men work the horses, and even ate with them. He felt bad about avoiding his friend, but if he stayed in the house one more day he thought he might end up yelling at him, and he wasn't sure that was the thing to do right now.

The next morning he rode to the Sheets place.

Everything Harry Sheets owned seemed a little bigger, a little cleaner, a little newer, and a little better than what

Carmichael had at his place. Clint was sure that was because everything at Carmichael's place had been built over a matter of years, while everything on the Sheets place had been built all at one time. While Carmichael had personally cut down all the timber he'd used to build his house, Clint was sure Sheets had bought all of his, and had someone build it for him.

He rode up to the house, and as was the case at his friend's place, men were working on the grounds; one came over to greet him.

"If you're lookin' for the boss he's in town," the man said.

"Who are you?"

"My name's Kane," the man said. "I'm the foreman."

"Would you tell Mrs. Carmichael I'm here to see her?" Clint asked.

"Mrs. Carmichael?"

"That's right," Clint said. "Elizabeth Carmichael?"

"Oh, you mean Betty? You a friend of hers?"

"Yes."

"That makes two of us," Kane said, with a wink that baffled Clint.

"Will you tell her I'm here?"

"Sure, sure," Kane said. "What's your name?"

"Clint Adams."

Kane frowned.

"I know that name, don't I?"

"Maybe."

Kane waited, but when Clint said nothing further, he said, "Wait here, I'll see if she's busy."

Clint wondered what Betty Carmichael would be busy doing. Was Sheets having her work on the spread?

Kane returned and said with a grin, "She's finishin' up. Just give her a minute or two. Go ahead in, the sitting room is to the right. She'll be down."

"Thanks."

"Want your horse cared for?"

"No," Clint said, "he'll be fine."

He grounded the reins and went up the steps to the door.

"Ain'tcha gonna tie your horse off?" Kane yelled.

"He's not going anywhere," Clint said, and went inside the house.

He turned right and found the sitting room. It was empty at the moment, furnished with plush furniture and curtains that carried a floral pattern. It didn't look like the sitting room of a rancher, but of a whorehouse.

He sat down on a sofa and, from where he was, could see the stairs. In a few minutes he heard someone coming down. A man appeared, donning a vest. He looked in at Clint, winked, and left. That was the second man who had winked at him. What the hell was going on?

After a few more minutes, he heard someone coming down the stairs more slowly. He waited and eventually Betty Carmichael appeared. She was wearing a filmy dressing gown and her hair was in a state of disarray. As she approached him Clint could see where Toby Carmichael might have thought she was beautiful. If she was forty-five she certainly had the high-breasted body of a much younger woman. Her face, however, looked haggard, the face of a forty-five-year-old woman who was very tired, and not the least bit happy.

"Betty?" he said.

"I'm ready," she said, "but you have to leave the money on the table there—"

"Betty?" he said again, louder, because she hadn't yet looked at him. "Betty, it's Clint Adams."

She hesitated, then lifted her head and looked at him.

"Clint? Is it really you?"

"Betty, what the hell is going on?"

"Oh, God," she said, covering her face, "I don't want you to see me like this."

A terrible realization came to him, one he was sure his conscious mind had been trying to deny. The winks, the looks, the way she looked, and her comment about putting

money on the table. Harry Sheets had her working as a
prostitute for his men.

"My God, Betty," he said, "what's he done to you?"

"Clint," she said, and fell against him, crying.

"We'd better go upstairs," he said. "We can talk alone
there."

They started out and she said, "Put some money on the
table, or someone will get suspicious."

He asked how much. She told him and he left it on the
table.

"Let's go upstairs," he said. "Show me your room."

"All right."

He followed her up the stairs, anxious to find out her
story. Why would she leave her husband to work for a man
who would pimp her out to his men? It didn't make sense—
unless she wasn't there willingly. Unless Toby Carmichael
was totally wrong about his wife leaving him for Harry
Sheets.

They went down a long hall and stopped at a door. She
looked at him before opening it.

"It's not pretty," she said.

"I don't care," he said, "I only want to talk."

She hesitated, then nodded and opened the door. She
went in and he followed. He stopped just inside the door,
stunned.

ELEVEN

Clint's memory of Betty Carmichael was of a beautiful, fastidious woman who kept her house immaculate. This room did not reflect that memory at all. It was filthy, stuffy, with food all around, dirty, soiled sheets that hadn't been changed in some time, and the air smelled of sex, both old and recent.

"Betty," Clint said, "you can't tell me you came here willingly."

She looked away.

"I came willingly, Clint," she said, "but I did not come to *this* willingly."

"What happened?"

"I was . . . tired of Toby. Have you seen him?"

"Yes."

"He changed," she said. "Not just physically, but . . . you see, I felt he was tired of *me*, so I left."

"And came here?"

"Yes."

"Why?"

"Because Harry Sheets was charming, handsome, exciting, and he said he loved me."

"How did this happen?"

"Once he got me into his house, he changed," she said.

43

"He said I had to take care of his men. I thought he meant cook for them, you know? But he meant . . . this."

"And how long have you been doing this?"

"Weeks."

Had he asked Carmichael how long she'd been gone? He didn't think so.

"When did you leave Toby?"

"The same time," she said, "just a few weeks ago."

"And this started right away?"

"Yes."

"Have you tried to get away?"

"I . . . thought about it, but . . ."

"But what?"

She looked at him, her eyes haunted and sad.

"Where would I go?"

"Where? Back to Toby."

"I couldn't!" she said. "I just couldn't. I'd be so ashamed."

"Go to the sheriff, then."

"He works for Harry."

"Well, you can't stay here," Clint said. "Now that I've seen you, I can't leave you here." He took her by the shoulders. "If you want to leave, Betty, I'll take you with me."

She hesitated only a moment, then said, "Oh, yes, Clint, yes."

"Do you have something else to put on?"

"I have one change of clothes," she said. "That's all Harry would allow me."

"Bastard," Clint said under his breath. "All right, you get changed. Are we in the back of the house?"

"Yes."

No point in looking out the window, then.

"Will his men try and stop us?"

"Oh, yes," she said, dropping her dressing gown to the floor unexpectedly. She was totally naked, her body pale, her breasts full and rounded. Apparently, she'd been at the mercy of these men for so long she thought nothing of being naked in front of Clint. However, she was still his friend's wife, so he turned his back to her.

"Then we won't have time to get you a horse," he said. "We'll both have to ride out on mine." Duke could carry them both for a while with no problem.

"A-all right," she said. "I'm ready."

He turned back. She was wearing a pair of dirty jeans, and a dirty man's shirt that she had to tie in a knot in front. On her feet were a pair of slippers.

"You have no boots?"

"No, this is all Harry would let me wear. He gave me these clothes so I could walk around the house when I wasn't . . . when there were no men . . . waiting . . ."

"Never mind," he said. "Come on, we're getting out of here."

They stepped out into the hall and went back down the stairs. Before they reached the bottom, Clint said, "Wait."

She remained on the stairs while he went down the rest of the way to make sure there were no men waiting in the sitting room. As a last thought he went and got his money off the table, then went back to the stairs.

"All right, come on."

They both went down the rest of the way and stopped just inside the front door. Clint looked out a front window and saw that Duke was still where he had left him. Further away some men were working with horses in a corral.

"I see five or six men," Clint said. "How many more will there be?"

"Probably nine," she said. "Harry took some into town with him, and the others are off working."

"Good," he said. "Five or six isn't too bad." He looked at her and added, "I want to do this without killing anyone, Betty."

"That suits me," she said, suddenly determined. "I just want to get away from here."

"Well," he said, "that's what we're going to do, right now."

TWELVE

Clint decided to go out the front door alone, descend the stairs and mount Duke. What happened next depended on, well, what happened next. There were plenty of scenarios to consider, but he decided not to do that. He decided to just do it.

So he walked down the steps and climbed up onto Duke's back. Before he could signal Betty to come out, though, the foreman, Kane, broke off from the other men and came over.

"All finished?"

"Yes."

"That quick?"

Clint just shrugged.

"I can send my men in now?"

Clint figured that Kane was thinking he'd been sent from town, probably from Sheets himself.

"Give her a few minutes to, you know, clean up," Clint said.

"That's funny," Kane said.

"What is?"

"A clean whore."

"Oh."

"I gotta get back to work."

47

"Thanks for letting me go in," Clint said.

"Forget it. Boss sent you, right?"

"That's right."

Kane shrugged, as if that said it all, turned, and went back to the corral.

Clint silently mouthed, "Come on," and waved at Betty to come.

If she'd done so immediately, they would have been home free, but she panicked. She hesitated, started out the door, stopped, then started again, and by that time one of the men had looked over.

"Hey!" he shouted.

"Come on!" Clint called.

Betty ran down the steps and reached up to Clint, who grabbed her arm and pulled her up behind him.

"Hey!" Kane yelled.

Clint wheeled Duke around and kicked him in the ribs to get him going.

"Hey, hey!" someone yelled. "He's stealin' our goddamned whore!"

Clint had to ride past the corral to get out and he drew his gun as he did. Breaking horses was hard work and men didn't usually wear guns while doing it. He didn't pause to see if he was right, though. He just threw a few shots their way and all of the men ducked.

Betty had her arms around Clint and was holding him so tightly he could hardly breathe.

"Direct me to town from here," he called.

She didn't answer. She had her face buried in his back, holding him even tighter, if that was possible.

"Betty! Come on!"

"What?"

"How do I get to town from here?" he asked. "Or do you want to go back to Toby?"

"No!" she said, her tone panicky. "We'll go to town."

•   •   •

Kane got to his feet and looked around.

"Nobody had a gun?"

The other five men shrugged and shook their head.

"Well, get one, and your horses."

"We goin' after them?" one of the men asked.

"You're damn right we are," Kane said. "The boss'll be real upset if we let her get away."

They all ran for bunkhouse to get their guns, and then to the barn for their horses.

That was when Kane remembered who Clint Adams was.

THIRTEEN

It was Clint's opinion that Betty should have gone back to Toby, but she wouldn't listen to that. She was sure Toby would never take her back, not after this. Clint remembered Toby calling her a slut and thought that maybe she was right.

In any case, they had to get ahold of some law, and the only way to do it was to go to town, use the telegraph, and send for some federal assistance, especially if—as Betty had told him—the law in Haywood was in Harry Sheets's pocket.

If the men from the Sheets spread were after them, Clint felt they had enough of a head start. They'd have to collect their guns and their horses before they chased them. That meant that he didn't have to push the big black gelding all that hard. When he felt they were far enough from the ranch, he slowed the horse down, and he and Betty were able to talk more easily.

"What do we do when we get to town?" she asked. "We can't go to the sheriff."

"Yes, we can."

"I told you, he works for Harry."

"And everyone knows it?"

"Well, no."

51

"Then he'll have to put up appearances for the town," Clint said. "We'll stop at the telegraph office first, though."

"What for?"

"To send for a U.S. Marshal."

"What then?"

"I'll have to keep you away from Harry Sheets until he gets here."

"That won't be easy," she said. "Harry doesn't like to lose what's his, and he has a lot of men working for him."

"If that's the case," Clint said, "then maybe Toby's our best chance."

"Why?"

"Because he's got men, too," Clint said. "You'd be safe there until I could get a marshal here."

Betty didn't speak.

"Also, they'll probably expect us to go to town."

"A-all right," she said. "Take me home, Clint."

"I'll need directions."

"We're actually closer to there than to town . . ."

Toby Carmichael was shocked to see Clint ride up to the house with Betty on the back of his horse, and was further shocked at her appearance when Clint lowered her to the ground.

"Toby—"

"What are you doin' here?" Carmichael demanded, cutting her off.

"Toby,—"

This time Clint cut her off.

"Betty, go inside and get freshened up. Let me talk to Toby."

"Clint—"

"Go on."

She obeyed, going into the house.

"I didn't want her in my house," Carmichael said.

"Why'd you bring her back here? I don't want her back here, Clint."

"Toby," Clint said, putting his arm around his friend's shoulders, "we have to talk."

They ended up in Carmichael's office, where Clint put the finishing touches on his story. He told his friend the truth.

"He made her a . . . a . . . *whore*?" Carmichael asked, incredulously.

"Forced her, Toby," Clint said. "Remember that part of it."

"A whore for *all* his men?" Carmichael continued, as if he hadn't heard Clint. "I don't want her here. She's probably diseased!"

"Toby," Clint said, "she's in trouble. She needs a place to stay, and somebody to protect her, until I can get a federal marshal here."

"Take her to the sheriff."

"The sheriff is in Harry Sheets's pocket."

"Did she lie with him, too?"

"Toby," Clint said, "you're not looking at the big picture here."

"What's the big picture?"

"I'm not saying you have to take her back for good," Clint said. "Just until I can do something about Harry Sheets."

"What are you gonna do?"

"What he did was illegal," Clint said. "You can't hold a woman against her will and force her to be a whore. He's going to have to pay for that."

Carmichael frowned and said, "I like that part. Keep talkin'."

"Just keep her here, and keep her safe, until I get back," Clint said. "I'll make her my responsibility, not yours."

"Why?" Carmichael asked. "Why would you help her?"

"That's simple," Clint said. "Because she needs help."

FOURTEEN

Carmichael finally agreed to keep Betty at the house until Clint got back. It helped that she came downstairs wearing one of her own dresses, fresh from a bath. She *looked* more like the Betty Carmichael her husband knew.

"What's going on?" she asked.

"You're going to stay here, Betty, until I get back," Clint said. "Toby and his men will protect you from Sheets and his men."

"I don't want anyone being killed over me," she said. "I'd go back there, first."

"You're not going back!" Carmichael growled. "Not to being a *whore*."

"Toby," Betty said, "can we talk?"

"Not now, Betty," Carmichael said. "You can stay here, but I can't talk to you now." He headed for the door, then stopped. "I have to talk to my men. They should have a say in this. I'll . . . be back."

He went out.

"How did you talk him into it?" she asked Clint.

"He wants to do it, Betty," Clint said. "He still loves you."

"I don't think so."

"You've got to give him some time to get over the shock of it," Clint said. "He'll come around."

"Clint," she said, "you know what I've been doing. . . . Toby, he's a good man. Did you know, that he's never been to a whore in his life?"

Clint did know that. Neither of them had ever paid for a whore, but for different reasons. Clint had *been* with whores, but he hadn't paid them. Carmichael had never even been with one. He considered them—untouchable.

"You know how he is," she went on. "He'll never touch me again."

"Maybe," Clint said. "We'll just have to wait and see."

"What are you going to do?"

"Go to town."

"Alone?"

"Yes."

"Shouldn't you take someone with you?"

"I want them all to stay here and take care of you," he said. "I'll be fine."

"Clint . . . I don't want you to get killed."

"I won't," he said. "I promise."

"How can you make a promise like that?"

"I've made a life out of keeping promises like that," he told her, "mainly to myself. Don't worry. I'll be back."

"I . . . don't know how to thank you."

"Don't worry about me," Clint said. "Think about what you're going to say to your husband."

Clint left the room, then went out the front door. On the porch, with the door closed behind him, he wondered how he would feel if he were married and found out that his wife had been with dozens of different men, dozens of times. Whether she was willing or not, that would not be an easy thing to forget.

He went down the stairs and grabbed Duke's reins. Carmichael came walking up to him at that moment.

"How did they take it?" Clint asked.

"I talked to Wade, he'll talk to the men. They didn't

sign on for gunplay. I won't blame them if they want to pull out.''

''Maybe I should stay around, see how many of them stay.''

''No, no, you go and do what you got to do,'' Carmichael said. ''There are enough of them who are loyal that I know I'll have enough men to stand Sheets off if he dares to come here.''

''His men will probably head for town first,'' Clint said. ''I'm going there now. By the time I get there he should know what's going on.''

''And then what?''

''And then he and I will have a talk.''

''What happens if he doesn't talk?'' Carmichael asked. ''What happens if he kills you?''

''If he kills me,'' Clint said, mounting up, ''this will be his next stop, and I'll have broken a promise I made to Betty. Why don't we wait and see if that happens?''

FIFTEEN

Clint rode into town slowly, giving the news time to get back to Harry Sheets. He didn't know where the man was. He was going to have to wait until Sheets came to him— or sent for him.

He brought Duke to the livery, where he instructed the liveryman to take care of him, but to be ready to saddle him at a moment's notice.

"You that feller?" the man asked.

"What fella?"

"The one what stole Harry Sheets's woman?"

"I didn't steal her," Clint said, "but yeah, I'm that fella."

"Reckon you won't be back, then," the older man said.

"I'll be back, my friend," Clint said. "You just see that you take care of my horse."

"Oh, I'll take care of 'im, mister," the man said. "You can count on that. That's my job."

"I will count on it, old-timer. You wouldn't happen to know where Harry Sheets is by any chance, would you?"

"My guess," the old man said, "would be the Stonegate Saloon."

"Stonegate?"

"Sheets owns it," the man said, "named it after some place he come from back East."

"Stonegate."

"That's the one."

"Much obliged."

"Don't thank me," the man said. "Chances are, you go over there, you ain't comin' back."

"You don't have much confidence in me, do you, old-timer?"

"Not against Sheets and his men," the man said, "I don't care if you was the Gunsmith hisself."

Clint decided to use this comment to his advantage.

"Well, then, I guess we're going to find out, aren't we?"

"Huh?"

"You see," Clint said, "I *am* the Gunsmith."

As he walked away, Clint heard the man talking to himself, scolding himself for not recognizing the big horse.

Clint found the Stonegate Saloon with no problem, and no help. It was easy. There were about a dozen horses tied up outside. Clint assumed that they belonged to the men from Harry Sheets's ranch, and that Sheets himself was probably inside.

He started for the saloon and then stopped. Instead, he decided to go and see the sheriff. Even if the man *was* in Sheets's pocket, it made sense to stop and fill him in first. Who knew, maybe he was looking for a way out of the rancher's pocket.

The sheriff's office was much like any other and the man was sitting behind his desk, drinking coffee and going through some wanted posters. Clint knew from experience that this was what lawmen did for most of their days.

"Sheriff?" Clint said, as he walked in.

"That's right, Sheriff Bascomb," the man said. "What can I do for you?"

Bascomb was in his forties and had probably been a lawman long enough to know how to play the game. This did not, however, necessarily mean that Betty was right and he was in the pocket of Harry Sheets.

"Sheriff, my name's Clint Adams."

"Adams," the man repeated, nodding. "I know the name. What brings you to town? Not trouble, I hope?"

"Well, actually, yes, that is what brings me to town," Clint said.

"What kind of trouble?"

"Harry Sheets."

"Sheets?"

"I understand you know him pretty well."

"I know most of the people around here pretty well," Bascomb said, carefully. "What kind of trouble do you have with Mr. Sheets?"

"Well, apparently he's been keeping a woman prisoner at his ranch so she could be a whore for his men."

Bascomb's first reaction was to laugh, but when he saw that Clint wasn't, he stopped short.

"You're joking."

"It's no joke."

Bascomb frowned. Clint couldn't tell whether or not the man knew what was going on.

"Who's the woman?"

"Betty Carmichael."

"Well, that explains it," Bascomb said, with apparent relief.

"Explains what?"

"You've made a mistake," the sheriff said.

"Have I?"

"Everyone hereabouts knows that Mrs. Carmichael left her husband for Harry Sheets."

"Maybe, but nobody knows what's been going on since then."

"And how do you know?"

"Because I went to see her," Clint said, "found out what was going on, and took her out of there."

"What?"

"That's where the trouble comes in," Clint said. "Sheets's men chased me, but lost me and came to town. I'm on my way to talk to Sheets now at his saloon."

"Talk to Mr. Sheets?"

"That's right," Clint said, "to find out his version of this whole thing. Would you care to come along and listen?"

"To talk to Mr. Sheets?" Bascomb repeated.

"That's right. After all, you *are* the law here. If he's been breaking the law you'll have to arrest him."

Bascomb swallowed, visibly shaken.

"Arrest Mr. Sheets?"

"That's right."

"I . . . don't know if I can do that."

"Why not?"

"Well . . . he's got a lot of men."

"Don't you have a deputy?"

"Well," Bascomb said, "at the moment, no."

"Well, come on over with me, then," Clint said. "I'll make sure nothing happens to you."

"Now wait a minute—"

"Or is what I heard about you true?"

Bascomb hesitated, then said, "I don't know what you've heard about me."

"That you're in Harry Sheets's pocket."

Clint waited for the man to deny it.

"Or maybe you are," he added, "but you don't want to be."

"When you're a town lawman," Bascomb said, carefully, "you sometimes have to . . . go along."

"Not with kidnapping a woman and forcing her to have sex for money," Clint said. "When you're a town lawman, you have to draw the line someplace."

Bascomb stared at Clint for a few moments without speaking.

"What about it, Sheriff?" Clint persisted. "Where do *you* draw the line?"

The sheriff looked undecided, as if he didn't know.

"Well, I'll be over at the saloon talking to Sheets," Clint said. "No matter what happens, I won't let him get away with doing that to Mrs. Carmichael anymore."

"Maybe . . ."

"Maybe what?"

"Maybe he . . . he wasn't forcing her."

Clint smiled tightly.

"I'm going to pretend you didn't say that, Sheriff," he said, "because Betty Carmichael is a friend of mine. I draw the line at people torturing my friends."

He turned and went to the door, opened it and looked at the sheriff.

"Like I said, let's find out where you draw yours."

SIXTEEN

When Clint approached the Stonegate Saloon, he saw all the horses that were tied off out front. No doubt they belonged to Harry Sheets's men, who were there giving him the bad news.

He stepped up onto the boardwalk and through the batwing doors. All conversation in the room stopped as all the men looked at him.

"That's him," someone said.

There was one man seated at a table as if he were sitting on a throne. He was in his late thirties by appearances, well dressed and carefully trimmed. There was a sweet, expensive scent in the air, and Clint had no doubt that it was coming from him.

"Send your men out, Sheets," Clint said. "This is between you and me."

"If you intend to kill me," Sheets said, "I'd prefer that they stay."

"If I intended to kill you," Clint said, "that would just get a bunch of them killed, too."

The men looked nervously at each other.

"But I don't intend to kill you, Sheets," Clint said, "just talk."

Sheets studied Clint for a few moments and then said to his men, "Wait outside, all of you."

It took a few moments for them to file out, but finally Clint and Sheets were alone in the room.

"Well," Sheets said, "I understand you have something that belongs to me."

"You have a lot of gall," Clint said, "I'll give you that."

"Gall? How's that?"

"To think that you can simply imprison a woman in your home, whore her out to your men."

"Imprison?" Sheets repeated, raising one eyebrow. "I'd hardly use that word. I gave Betty Carmichael a place to stay."

"Maybe it started out that way."

"She didn't do anything she didn't want to do."

"I don't think that's quite the case."

Sheets looked . . . put out.

"Really, Adams, this is none of your affair."

"I'm making it my affair," Clint said. "Both of the Carmichaels are friends of mine."

"I have no objection to Betty seeing old friends," Sheets said, spreading his soft, manicured hands in a magnanimous gesture.

"Whatever objections you have or don't have are of no concern anymore, Sheets. Betty is not coming back to your house."

"Well," Sheets said, "Whatever you think, Adams, that is just a minor inconvenience. Actually, I really don't care whether she comes back or not. She can be replaced."

"By another woman you'll hold prisoner?"

Sheets frowned now, to show he was annoyed.

"Now, that *is* none of your business," he said. "What I do or don't do in my own home—"

"When it hurts other people, Sheets, yes, what you do in your home concerns me."

"Nevertheless," Sheets continued, "the matter of Betty

Carmichael is closed. Tell her I no longer need her. She can stay with her husband or go wherever she wants to go. However, she may not return to my home.''

"And why would she want to?''

Sheets smiled and said, "Why, indeed. Are we finished, Mr. Adams?''

"We are," Clint said, "for now." He turned and left.

Outside, the men were milling about, but when Clint came out they spread out to give him room to pass. As Clint walked away from the saloon he saw the sheriff coming toward him.

"You're too late," he said.

"I didn't hear a shot," the lawman said. "You didn't—"

"No," Clint said, "I didn't."

"Then what happened?''

"We talked.''

"And?''

"And Betty Carmichael is free to make her own decision about what she wants to do.''

"Wasn't she always?''

"I told you," Clint said, "she was a prisoner. As far as I'm concerned, you should go in there and arrest Sheets for kidnapping.''

"I'd have to hear it from her," the sheriff said.

"If I have anything to say about it," Clint said, "you will.''

"I won't.''

Clint looked at Toby Carmichael, who shook his head and shrugged.

"Why not?" Clint asked. "He held you prisoner, Betty, made you do things—''

"I won't talk to the law," she said, shaking her head. "That's final.''

"Then I will," Clint said.

"What will that accomplish?" Carmichael asked.

"I don't know," Clint said, "but I can't let Sheets get

away with this. He'll just do it to someone else.''

"I'm going to go to my room," Betty said, and went back upstairs.

"What are you going to do?" Carmichael asked.

"I'm sending a telegram to the capital," Clint said. "Maybe they'll send a marshal here to look into it. What about you?"

"Me?"

"You and Betty."

"I don't know that there is a me and Betty," Carmichael said, "but she can stay here until she makes up her mind what she wants to do."

"I hope it works out between you," Clint said.

"I don't see how it could," Carmichael said. "All those men . . ."

Clint didn't know what to say to his friend, except good-bye. . . .

That had been weeks ago. Clint had done as he'd said he would. He sent a telegram, hoping that a federal marshal would be dispatched to look into the actions of Harry Sheets.

So was that what this was all about? Did these men who were chasing him work for Harry Sheets? There were two ways to find out. One was to ask them, but if he got close enough to them they were going to shoot him.

The other way was to ask Harry Sheets.

SEVENTEEN

Once Clint crossed back into New Mexico, he was sure he had lost his pursuers for good. The only way they'd find him now was if they *were* from Haywood and in the employ of Harry Sheets, because that was where he was going.

He didn't know what difference a few weeks had made in Haywood. Maybe Toby and Betty Carmichael had reconciled. Maybe Harry Sheets had been investigated and arrested by a federal marshal.

Or maybe there was no difference at all.

He didn't know how wrong he was.

When he arrived in Haywood, he decided to stop at the sheriff's office first, before talking to either the Carmichaels or Harry Sheets. Maybe the lawman could give him an idea of what was going on.

When he entered the sheriff's office the man looked up at him, surprised, and said, "How did you know?"

"What?"

"Did you see it in the newspapers?"

"I didn't see anything," Clint said. "What are you talking about?"

Sheriff Bascomb stood up and fidgeted nervously.

"What's going on, Sheriff?"

69

"None of it was my fault," the lawman said. "I want you to know that."

"None of what?"

"The killings."

"What killings?"

Bascomb took a deep breath and then said, "Your friend, Toby Carmichael, he killed them."

"Killed who?"

"His wife," the sheriff said, "and Harry Sheets."

"What?" Clint sank into a chair. "When? What the hell happened?"

"After you left—days after you left—she went back to him."

"Back to who? Sheriff, sit down, relax, and tell me the story."

The sheriff took a deep breath, sat back down, and started talking. . . .

After Clint left town, Betty Carmichael went back to Harry Sheets, back to being a whore for his men—and she went back willingly. No one in town could explain it, or understand it—or *believe* it—but she went back. It took a few more days after that, but apparently Toby Carmichael went over there one night and shot and killed both of them.

"That's when the federal marshal got to town, and he took Carmichael into custody."

"The marshal didn't arrive until then?"

"He said he'd been sent here in response to your telegram, so he just happened to be here to arrest Carmichael."

"But how—"

"Carmichael came to town—came here—and told me and the marshal that he'd killed his wife and Harry Sheets."

"What about Sheets's men?"

"They were in town, most of them, when it happened."

"I can't believe this. Where's Toby now?"

Bascomb looked away.

"Sheriff?"

"He's dead."

"*What?*" Clint said. "Did you have a trial and hang him already?"

"Didn't have to," Bascomb said. "He hung himself in his cell." He opened a desk drawer, took out a newspaper, and put it on the desk.

"It's all there," he said. "Our newspaper editor interviewed the marshal, who laid it all out for him."

Clint took the newspaper and read it. The marshal explained it in the paper just as the sheriff had explained it to him. Carmichael, in a fit of rage and jealousy, killed both his wife and Harry Sheets. After he was incarcerated, in a fit of depression, he hung himself with his belt.

Clint put the paper back on the table.

"I thought you came because you heard . . ." Bascomb said.

"No," Clint said, shocked not only by the actions of his friend, but by all three deaths. "No, I came to talk to Sheets."

"About what?"

Clint told Bascomb about the men who had attacked him, tracking him to three Arizona towns.

"Sheets has been dead for weeks," Bascomb said when Clint finished. "Why would his men attack you?"

"I don't know," Clint said. "I guess I was wrong. It has to be something else."

"With your reputation," Bascomb said, "it could be anything."

Clint hated to admit it, but the lawman might be right.

As he stood up, Bascomb asked, "What are you going to do?"

"Be on my way," Clint said. "I guess my curiosity will have to go unsatisfied."

"Unless those men find you and try again," the lawman said.

"Yes," Clint said, "unless that happens . . ."

EIGHTEEN

Jenny Hart was sweet.

She was sweet all over.

The skin of her breasts was soft, smooth, and sweet, and the pink nipples were like hard little raisins. The flesh on the insides of her thighs was soft and also sweet, and when his tongue entered her she was the sweetest of all.

Clint turned Jenny over and began to kiss her butt. Even the skin there was sweet, and sweeter still as his tongue moved into the crease between her buttocks, where some of the sweet moistness of her had collected during their long night of lovemaking.

He kept his weight on his arms and knees and hovered over her, running the length of his penis over her buttocks, and then he slid himself between her legs, rubbing himself on the soft skin of her thighs. Finally, she got to her knees, giving him the signal to go further. She lifted her butt to him and he slid up and into her from behind. She groaned as he entered her, as the long length of him invaded her insides, slid in and out of her easily, wetly.

"Clint," she said, moaning, "you promised . . . you promised . . ."

73

He did promise, and he intended to keep his promise because he didn't encounter that many woman who liked to have sex this way.

He withdrew from her, huge and glistening from her wetness. She spread her legs and lifted her butt, and he pressed the head of his penis against her tight, brown little hole and pushed. He entered her gently at first, until he was all the way in, and then he began to move, aided by the sheen of her.

"Oooh, yes," she moaned, biting her lower lip, "oh God, yes . . . now the rest . . ."

For the rest, he reached around her with one hand, found her moist slit, and slid one finger inside of her, so that he was now inside her front and back. He slid his finger in and out as he continued the motion behind her, and then he slid his finger up until he encountered her stiff little clit and that was the trigger. She began to buck against him, gasping and groaning. She'd told him that she loved it this way and, during the night, had made him promise to take her like this before they were done.

He was keeping his promise and was damn glad he was. She had ahold of him now, tightening on him and pulling on him while he manipulated her. Finally, when he could hold back no more, he groaned aloud and ejaculated into her, sending her into a new series of frenzied movements, pulling still more out of him, milking him until there was no more to milk—and still she wanted more and refused to let him go . . .

"You tried to kill me," he said, later.

"I tried to make sure you'd remember me after you left this morning," she said. "That's all."

They had met in the saloon where she worked, began to talk and realized they were attracted to each other. After he made sure she knew that he never paid for a woman, she agreed to come to his room with him since he'd only be in town for one night.

"A night to remember," she had said, and she was right.

"Well," he said, "you succeeded in that."

She moved up so she was leaning on his chest and kissed him soundly.

"I have to thank you," she said. "I haven't done it that way in a long time, and you're the first man in a while I could even talk to about it."

"If there's anything I want to do with a beautiful woman," he said, "it's give her what she wants."

"And you did *that*," she said.

She slid off his chest and lay next to him, on her stomach. She had an exquisite ass, high and round and smooth, supple yet firm—and, like the rest of her, sweet.

He wondered if he should squeeze one more day out in Temple, Nebraska, then decided not. It would probably be impossible to duplicate the night they just had; trying to might end up disappointing, and ruin the memory of this one.

"If you're thinking about staying," she said into the pillow, "don't. It would ruin everything."

"How did someone so young get so smart?" he asked.

She turned her head to look at him and smile.

"I'm thirty . . . something, which is not so young. And I don't know how smart I am, or I'd be in a house with a picket fence and not working in a saloon."

"Is that what you want?" he asked. "A house with a picket fence?"

"Are you offering?"

"No."

"Well," she said, rolling onto her back, "it's probably not what I really want, either."

Clint had probably had this talk with dozens of women over the years, but he'd never had time to get deeper into it with them, to find out what they truly wanted. His own truth was he rarely stayed in one place long enough to find out.

And that included now.

NINETEEN

He was about three hours out of Temple when he heard the first shot. He turned in his saddle and saw six men riding toward him. One had fired, and now the others fired, as well.

"Not again," he said, and kicked Duke in the ribs to get him going.

The chase went on for some time, with the six men firing, reloading, and firing again. Only six this time, he told himself, not twelve like the last, but there was a pony in the front with some distinctive spottings that he recognized. At least one of these men had been with that first group.

He began to outdistance them again, but he kept his eyes peeled for the other six men. Maybe they would appear in front of him. Maybe somebody had gotten smart and decided to flank him. But as the chase went on, it became apparent that was not the case. Six more men did not appear, and he continued to put space between himself and these six.

This was not satisfactory to him, however. Ever since the first incident two months ago he'd been thinking about it, wondering who the men were, why they were after him, trying to come up with an answer. This time he decided he would do something to try and find out.

He was riding through familiar territory, riding south, back the way he had come earlier that week. He remembered the terrain and was trying to pick out a place where he might get the drop on six men. It was risky, but it was all he could think of. He could have done it with a rifle from higher ground, but that wasn't what he wanted. He wanted to be close enough to speak to them, question them, find out what this was all about.

He finally remembered a place that might serve his purpose. It was a rock formation that they would either have to ride around or through. He'd leave a clear trail so that they'd ride through. Once they were among the rocks, they'd have to slow down so that their horses wouldn't throw a shoe or break a leg. There was a place where he would be able to get the jump on them, close up, with his pistol. If they knew who he was, his appearance with a gun in his hand might give them pause—and why would they be so intent on chasing him, and shooting at him, if they didn't know who he was?

He was going to count on his reputation—something he rarely did—to help him control them . . . hopefully without having to kill any of them.

TWENTY

When Clint was in position, he felt better. He was doing something, not just running, the way he had two months ago. Of course, then it had been a dozen men; and reputation or no reputation, he wasn't about to face down a dozen men alone. Six . . . well, that wasn't going to be easy, either, but it was a hell of a lot better than twelve.

He could hear the horses approaching, hear their shoes scraping the rocks beneath them. The men were riding carefully or, if they were smart, they were walking their horses through the rocks. Clint hoped for the latter. It would be easier if they were walking, concerning themselves with their horses, when he got the drop on them.

When he saw the first man he realized he had lucked out. The man was on foot. Soon the second appeared, and then the third, and then all of them, on foot, walking single file.

Single file, that was a problem. That meant there were at least five horse lengths separating the first and last man. If he covered the first, the last man might try something, and vice versa. He had to make up his mind quickly which way he was going to play it.

If he'd picked a higher vantage point he could have covered all six, but he was only about ten feet above them. Too low to cover a five-length spread.

He had a bad feeling about how this was going to turn out, but he'd come too far to quit now.

He decided to stop them when the third man's horse was right in front of him. That would put him about the same distance from the first as the last.

He waited behind the rock; and when the third man was going past, he jumped up on top of it, holding his gun at the ready.

"Just stand easy, boys, and nobody will—"

They reacted too quickly, even before he could finish his little speech. Two of the men in front and one in back went for their guns. The other three froze. That was what saved their lives.

Instinct worked in Clint's favor. Without thinking, he swung toward the first two men and fired twice. The third man, the one all the way in back, fired but missed, and Clint turned on him and fired before the man could squeeze the trigger of his own gun again.

There were now three dead men, and three live ones. The three horses belonging to the dead men spooked and, having no one to hold them, took off. The remaining three men held their horses in check.

The first man killed, the man at the head of the column, had been riding the pony with the distinctive markings. Clint hoped that he had not been the only one who had ridden with the first group.

"You three want to try your luck?" he asked.

Two of the men shook their heads, but the third asked, "You carry five shots in that gun, or six?"

"What do you care?" Clint asked. "The fourth shot is yours."

Clint waited to see if the man wanted to try. Their body language said no as they moved their hands away from their guns.

"That's good," Clint said. "Now, toss your guns away— left-handed . . . except for you, Lefty," he added to the man who'd spoken, "you do it right-handed."

All three men obeyed and tossed their guns away.

"Now, let go of your horse's reins. You won't be needing them."

They all hesitated, but complied.

"Smack their rumps."

"You gonna leave us afoot?" one of them asked.

"You're alive, aren't you?" Clint asked. "Besides, they won't go far in these rocks. Go on, do it."

Again, they hesitated, but obeyed. Their horses moseyed off lazily.

"Now move closer together, arm's length from one another."

They did so.

"What are you gonna do?" Lefty asked. He was the man who had been concerned with how many shots Clint carried in his gun.

"We're going to have a talk."

"About what?"

"About why you're chasing me, so intent on killing me," Clint said.

"You mean you don't know?" one of the other men asked.

"I don't see any badges on you, so you're not a deputized posse."

The three men remained silent.

"Well? Who wants to go first? Why are you after me?"

"Mister," Lefty said, "we don't know. We just hired on."

"You mean you were chasing me, and shooting at me, without knowing why?"

Lefty shrugged and said, "We was being paid."

"By who?"

"Him," Lefty said, indicating the first dead man.

"He was riding with about eleven other men a couple of months ago, all trying to shoot me. Were any of you with them?"

"Hell, no," Lefty said. "We just signed on a few days ago."

"If you're lying—"

"How you gonna tell if we're lyin'?" Lefty asked.

"You're right," Clint said. "I can't tell, so I might as well just shoot you now."

"We ain't lyin', mister," one of the other men said, "honest, we ain't. We just hired on, like Lefty said."

Clint supressed a laugh at finding out that Lefty was "Lefty's" real name.

"Where?"

"In Temple."

"And he hired you?" Clint asked, indicating the dead man.

"That's right," Lefty said.

"What's his name?"

"Harley," Lefty said.

"Last name?"

"We don't know."

"None of you knew him?"

"Never saw him before," Lefty said.

"What about the three of you? You know each other?"

"To nod at," Lefty said. "I knew Winston—he's back there, the third one you killed."

"And you fellas?"

"Didn't know nobody," one of them said, and the other nodded.

"So you're not from Temple?"

"Them two were," Lefty said, indicating the other two dead men. "Not the rest of us."

"So you can't tell me why you were after me?"

"Hell," Lefty said, "we thought sure you'd know that."

"Well, I don't," Clint said. "Any of you fellas know my name?"

The three of them shook their head.

"My name's Clint Adams."

They all stared at him, bug-eyed.

"You know who I am?"

"We s-sure do, Mr. Adams," Lefty said. "Hell, if we'd knowed it was you we wouldn't—"

"If anyone else hires you, or you hear of anyone else hiring on, you tell them who they're after, you hear?"

"We sure will, sir," one of the others said.

"And if I find out any of you were lying, I'll come looking for you."

"We ain't lyin', Mr. Adams," Lefty said, "not to you."

"Then get out of here," Clint said. "Start walking back to Temple."

Lefty started to lean over to retrieve his gun.

"Leave the guns."

"It's dangerous out here—"

"More dangerous if you try to pick up a gun," Clint said. "Get!"

The three men turned and started back through the rocks as fast as they could go. If they wanted their horses, they'd have to circle around to find them. Clint felt sure they'd be more concerned with putting some distance between them and him.

He watched them from his rock; when they were out of sight, he dropped to the ground.

TWENTY-ONE

Keeping alert, in case the three men did decide to come back, Clint set about searching the three dead men for clues as to who sent them after him. He saved the leader for last.

A search through the pockets of the first two dead men yielded nothing but fifty dollars each. He wondered if his life was going that cheaply, or if that was all they had left of what they'd been paid.

Finally, he searched the leader, whose horse he had recognized. This man was carrying two hundred dollars, and a letter from a law firm in San Francisco. The letter stated simply that they—the firm of Barkley, Cartwright, and Lancer—were expecting that he—Harley Samuels—was bringing the "matter" to a satisfactory close. The letter finished by saying they were expecting to hear from him. It was signed "Richard Barkley."

Clint didn't know a Richard Barkley, nor did he know anyone named Cartwright or Lancer. For that matter, he didn't even know if he was the "matter" the letter was referring to. But this was the only clue he had and he intended to follow it up.

He folded the letter and put it in his pocket. He let each man hold onto his money, not that it was going to do them any good where they were going. Briefly, he considered

leaving them where they lay, but in the end he decided to
bury them. That meant dragging them away from the rocks
until he found ground soft enough to dig three graves.
However, as he was digging the first one he decided that
they didn't deserve to have their own holes, so he dug it
deeper, dropped them all into the same hole, and covered
it up.

That done, he fetched Duke, mounted up, and rode after
the horses which had been spooked by the shooting. He
decided not to chase the other five, but he did run down
the sixth—the pony with the distinctive markings—and
went through the saddlebags he assumed belonged to the
dead man named Harley Samuels.

He found nothing but some extra shirts and an extra gun
that needed a new firing pin. He dropped the saddlebags
onto the ground, unsaddled the horse, and slapped him on
the rump. He'd either like being free, or wander back to
the town of Temple. Either way Clint was done here.

Now it was on to San Francisco.

TWENTY-TWO

Clint had made many trips to San Francisco, and for a while he would stay in the same place each time. However, the bigger his reputation got, the more dangerous this became. The last thing he wanted to be was predictable. So over the past five or six years, whenever he came to town, he stayed at a different hotel. He also tried to stay away from the larger Portsmouth Square hotels. Not because they were expensive, but because so many people stayed at them because of the gambling.

This time he found a small hotel further from the Square than he was used to staying. He did this because he did not want to be recognized—especially on this trip.

Once he was in his room, he took out the letter again, the one from the law firm of Barkley, Cartwright and Lancer. He read it for the umpteenth time, but it yielded nothing further. All he knew were these three lawyers' names and that their office was on Market Street.

He needed to talk to someone who knew what was going on in the city. This was a small list—probably three men—and he chose the one he thought he could trust the most: a man named Duke Farrell.

Duke ran a hotel in partnership with another man, who used it as a base of operations but was rarely around. Actually, Duke *owned* it together with the man, but virtually ran the place on his own.

However, Clint didn't want to meet Duke at his hotel, as it catered to a clientele that included the famous and infamous. Instead, he sent a message with a young boy, asking Duke to meet him in a saloon on the Barbary Coast called The Bucket of Blood. He simply signed the note "Clint," figuring Duke would know who it was from.

Clint got a cold beer with nothing floating in it from the bartender and grabbed a back table. It was early in the day and The Bucket of Blood was almost empty. Clint was glad of this when he saw Duke enter, wearing a suit that would have caught the eye of everyone in the place if it were full and probably cause trouble. As it was, the bartender was giving Duke the eye as the man walked to Clint's table.

Clint stood and shook hands with Duke. At five foot six, the man was half a foot shorter than Clint, but about the same age.

"I knew it had to be you," Duke said, sitting. "Nobody else would have the nerve to pick this place."

"That's why I picked it," Clint said. "I don't want to be seen. You want a beer?"

"Here?" Duke asked. "You've got to be joking. Come on, Clint, what's on your mind? I don't want to be here when the workday ends and it starts to fill up."

"I need some information."

"What kind?"

"The quiet kind."

"About who?"

"A law firm called Barkley, Cartwright and Lancer," Clint said.

Duke made a face.

"You know them?"

"I know the firm," Duke said. "They do a lot of work for the high society types. At least, that's the aboveboard work they do."

"And?" Clint pressed.

"Nobody knows about their other clients."

"The low society type?"

"The lowest."

"That might explain a lot."

"About what?"

Clint told Duke his story, about the dozen riders who tried to ride him down, and then the half dozen two months later.

"And you think those incidents are connected? You got a lot of people out there who would want a piece of you, Clint."

"The same man was with both groups."

"And what did he have to say?"

"He wasn't talking the last time I saw him."

"Oh."

"But he had this letter in his pocket."

Clint took the letter out and handed it across to the smaller, more dapper man. Duke read it and passed it right back.

"What do you want to know?"

"Well, part of what I want to know you already told me," Clint said. "This is the type of firm who would broker a killing."

"In a second," Duke said, "but it would cost a lot of money. Who do you know who wants you dead, and can afford them?"

"That's for me to find out."

"And me?"

"See if you can find out what's been going on inside the firm," Clint said.

"What, specifically, do you want to know?"

"Maybe one of the partners specializes in these matters?" Clint asked. "Maybe one man in particular is the broker. If you can find that out, I can have a talk with him. If not, I'll have to try to talk to all three."

"All right," Duke said, "I'll see what I can do for you. Where are you staying?"

Clint told him.

"Why don't you come and stay with us?"

"Like I said," Clint told him, "I don't want to be seen. I'll stay where I am for a while."

"Suit yourself," Duke said. "I'm gonna get out of this place and off the Barbary Coast while I'm still in one piece." He stood up. "I'll be in touch when I know something."

Clint stood and the two men shook hands. He remained standing until Duke left the place, then sat back down to finish his beer and mull over some of what he'd just found out.

TWENTY-THREE

Clint stayed in The Bucket of Blood a little too long. The regular clientele starting filing in—longshoremen, sailors, and the like. He could tell they were asking the bartender about him, but nobody was approaching him to start trouble. This made him suspicious, and curious. Suspicious that somebody in the place knew who he was, and curious about who it could be.

It occurred to him that with the law firm brokering killings for hire, this would be one of the spots they'd come to look for likely hires. Of course, they'd have their regulars, and maybe Harley Samuels was one of those, but if the regulars needed help, this was the kind of place they'd come to.

He didn't doubt that there were men in the place right at that moment who had killed, and done it for money.

He watched as a newcomer came in, saw Clint sitting at the back table, and then went to the bartender to ask who he—the legitimate newcomer—was. Clint realized then that it had to be the bartender who recognized him. If that was the case, then he was in a room full of cutthroats and murderers—not to mention shanghaiers—who knew who he was.

That was good news and bad news.

The good news was they knew who he was and would probably leave him alone.

The bad news was they knew who he was and, sooner or later, somebody would come in—or somebody would get drunk enough—to want to try him.

It was time to leave—but his decision came moments too late.

As he was finishing his beer he saw two burly men walking over to his table. They were obviously dockworkers, judging from their clothes and their general appearance.

"Hey, friend," one of them said loudly, so others in the room could hear him.

"You talking to me?" Clint asked.

"Yeah, you," the man said. "You're sitting at our table."

"Yeah," the other man added, "our table."

"Oh," Clint said, standing, "sorry. You can have it. I didn't know it belonged to anybody."

The two men exchanged a glance. Obviously, they had expected to provoke him and were puzzled by his reaction.

"Can I buy you gents a beer to make up for it?" Clint asked.

"Buy us a beer?" the first one asked. "You think you can get off just with buying us a beer?"

"Oh, sorry," Clint said. "I didn't mean to insult you. How about I buy you both dinner?"

Again the two men exchanged a glance.

"What do you say?" Clint asked. "I can't stay and eat with you, but I'll stand you to a—"

"What the hell's the matter with you, mate?" the first man cut in.

"Sorry?"

"Why are you so damn polite?" the man asked. "We're takin' the table away from you and you wanna buy us dinner? I thought you was some kind of legend."

"Who told you that?"

"The bartender," the man said. "Said he recognized you and you were some legend, some Gun . . . guy."

"Guess he must be wrong," Clint said. "Sorry I'm not your . . . guy."

Clint turned and started to leave. He was almost to the door and thought he'd made it when the man called, "Hey, what are ya, yella?"

He heard the footsteps as the two burly dockworkers charged at him from behind. He didn't have the time, and he sure as hell did not have the inclination to try and beat both of them in a fight, so he turned, drew his gun, and stuck it into the mouth of the nearest man. Unfortunately for him that man was still moving at the time, so the barrel of the gun shattered some teeth on the way in.

"Whaffa—" the man started, his eyes wide.

Clint cocked the hammer back on the gun and the man quieted down.

"Right now you got some broken teeth, friend," Clint said. "You want to try for an exploding head?"

The man's eyes bugged out and he shook his head just a bit, not wanting to make Clint's gun go off.

"How about you?" Clint asked the other man. "Want to see your friend's head explode?"

"Hey, no," the man said, "we was just havin' fun—"

"I don't have time for your kind of fun," Clint said. "I'm going to ease my gun out of your friend's mouth and leave. If I was you, I'd forget all about having some fun and take him to a doctor."

"Sure, mister, s-sure."

Clint eased his gun out of the man's mouth, and blood dribbled down his chin. He paused to clean the blood from the gun barrel on the man's shirt, then eased the hammer off and holstered it.

He looked over at the bartender and said, "I owe you anything for drinks?"

"Not a thing," the man said.

Clint took a few coins from his pocket and flipped them to the bartender one by one. The man deftly caught each coin in one hand.

"Drinks for the house," he said, and left.

TWENTY-FOUR

Clint went back to his hotel, hoping that the incident at the Barbary Coast would not get around. At least he'd gotten away without firing a shot. That surely would have spread the word that he was in San Francisco. As it was, the bartender with the big mouth might do it alone, depending on the size of his clientele.

He checked at the desk for messages, even though the only one who would be leaving him one would be Duke. The clerk apologized and said there was nothing there. He called Clint "Mr. Hartman" because Clint had registered under his friend Rick Hartman's name. It had been the only other name he could think of when he checked in, other than his own. It didn't really matter, though, since Rick was in Labyrinth, Texas.

He went up to his room and looked down at the street. The gaslights were lit and it was almost fully dark. He liked San Francisco at this time of night, maybe more than any other city. Of course, he liked spending time in Portsmouth Square. The Square had a pulse, but it was a pulse he had to keep his finger off of this trip—at least, until he found out what he wanted to know.

He thought about leaving the room and going to a saloon but in the end he decided why take the chance. Instead he removed his boots and lay down on the bed for a nap.

When he opened his eyes it was morning.

When Clint went down to the hotel dining room for breakfast he felt rotten. He had slept for twelve hours. He *hated*
sleeping that long because instead of being well-rested, it
made him feel sluggish, which was why he hadn't done it
in years.

"What will you have, Mr. Hartman?" the waiter asked.

It took Clint almost a full minute to realize the man was
talking to him.

"How do you know my name?" he asked.

"It's a little trick of mine," the waiter said. "I find out
the names of new guests. I'm just . . . well, trying to make
your stay more pleasant."

And angling for some kind of a tip, no doubt, Clint
thought.

"Steak and eggs," he said, "some spuds, biscuits, and
coffee. Lots of coffee."

"I'll bring one of our large pots sir."

"Thank you."

Clint looked around the room at the other diners, found
that no one was paying particular attention to him except
for a woman who was sitting alone. She was about thirty,
very attractive, with black hair worn clipped up at the back
of her head in pretty curls, and a conservative skirt that
nevertheless showed a little bit of her ankles. She smiled
at him and he smiled back, but it was too early in the
morning for much of anything else. She looked as if she
was dressed either for shopping or for business.

The waiter brought the coffee first, and Clint asked if he
could find him a newspaper.

"Right away, sir."

The man brought him that day's copy of the *San Francisco Chronicle*, and Clint started to read and drink coffee
while he waited for his breakfast.

"Excuse me?"

He lowered the paper and saw the woman standing in front of his table.

"Hello," he said. It was all he could think of at the moment.

"I'm sorry to bother you," she said, "but . . . this is embarrassing."

"What is?"

"Well, I don't usually ask strange men for money, but—"

"Is there a problem?"

"I left my money in my room, and I don't want to sound like I'm trying to get out of paying for my breakfast. You're staying in the hotel, aren't you?"

"That's right."

"Well, so am I. I'm in room two thirteen."

"I'm in two twenty-four."

He was still groggy from too much sleep, and wasn't even sure of what he was saying.

"I wonder if you could loan me the money to pay for my breakfast? I would be in your debt. I could pay you back later today . . ."

Clint studied her, and wondered if she was trying to scam him for the cost of a meal. It didn't seem likely, but then, most good con women did not look like con women.

"Well . . ."

"How about this? Don't give me the money, just pay for mine when you pay for yours. I swear, I'll make it up to you . . . later."

"Can I ask a question?"

"Of course," she replied.

"Why me?"

"Well . . . you're alone, and most of the men here aren't—and the one's that *are* don't look friendly."

"And I do?"

"Extremely."

"All right," he said. "You go and do what you have to do today and I'll take care of your breakfast."

"Really? Oh, that's wonderful. It will save me some real embarrassment."

"Well," Clint said, "I wouldn't want you to be embarrassed."

"I'm really in your debt. Oh, by the way my name is Chyna."

"China?"

"With a 'y,' " she said. "Chyna Delaney."

"Pleased to meet you, Chyna," he said. "I'm—"

"I asked the waiter who you were," she said. "I can't thank you enough, Mr. Hartman, and I know we'll be seeing each other again . . . real soon."

He started to correct her about his name, but she suddenly turned and hurried out of the dining room. He figured that was better, anyway. He really didn't want anyone to know who he was, not even a pretty girl who had just become in debt to him.

The waiter returned with his breakfast, and after he had out it down, Clint said, "By the way, I'll be taking care of Miss Delaney's breakfast bill, as well."

"Yes, sir," the waiter said, with a smile that was more of a smirk. "As you wish."

Clint set to his breakfast, thinking that it would be interesting to find out if he had really been scammed by a pretty face—and ankles—or not.

TWENTY-FIVE

Clint paid the bill after breakfast—his bill and Chyna Delaney's bill—and couldn't stop himself from going to the front desk to check and see if she really was a guest at the hotel. As it turned out, she was. Now it just remained to be seen if she was going to pay him back, or make it up to him, somehow.

After that he was at somewhat of a loss as to how to spend the day. He was still determined to stay away from Portsmouth Square—even in the daytime—because that was where he usually spent most of his time when he was in San Francisco. There was always the chance that he'd be recognized.

The Barbary Coast was out, because he'd already been there and had already been recognized.

The part of San Francisco he rarely went to was its business district, where the law firm of Barkley, Cartwright and Lancer had their offices.

That was where he decided to go, just to have a look.

The cab he'd hailed in front of his hotel dropped him on Market Street, several doors down from the building where the law firm had its offices. He'd been to Market Street before, but doubted that there was a chance he'd be recognized.

He crossed to the other side of the street and took up a place in what looked to be a seldom-used doorway. From this vantage place he could see the front door of the building that housed the law firm. He didn't know what he was looking for, however. What were the chances that someone he knew or recognized would go in or come out of the building? And if someone did, what were the chances they were going to or coming from the offices of that law firm? There were a lot of things that could happen that could be coincidence—if he believed in them.

He decided that if someone he recognized went in or came out, they *were* going to the offices of Barkley, Cartwright and Lancer, the firm that had brokered the attempts on his life.

He remained in that doorway for a couple of hours, and began to try to come up with a scheme that would get him a look at the three members of the law firm.

He considered the wisdom of going up to the office and acting as a prospective client, but he had no way of knowing if the members of the firm knew what the victims of their "brokered" killings looked like.

Finally, after a couple more hours, he decided to go back to his hotel. There was nothing he could do here until Duke Farrell told him which member of the law firm was the actual broker, and what he looked like. That was when he'd take action.

He started to step from the doorway when a cab pulled up in front of the building across the street and a woman got out. He immediately recognized the ringlets of hair on the woman's head. He watched as Chyna Delaney paid her fare and then went into the building.

Now *there* was a coincidence that was undeniable, even for him.

He settled back into the doorway to wait for the woman to come out.

She reappeared in just under an hour, and he realized his mistake. He should have had a cab waiting so that he could follow her if she hailed one. Luckily, at that moment, she did not seem interested in hailing a cab. Instead she looked both ways, then turned left and began to walk up the street. He quit his doorway, remained on the other side of the street, and began to follow.

He followed her for several blocks until she ducked into another building. This was also a building that housed businesses. He waited until she was inside, then crossed the street. He checked the lobby of the building to be sure whether she was there or not. When he saw that it was empty, he went inside. On the wall was a directory listing the businesses that maintained offices in the building. It was an alphabetical listing and he didn't recognize any of the names until he got to the letter ''P.''

The building was the home of the San Francisco offices of the Pinkerton Detective Agency.

The coincidences were getting worse and worse. What were the chances that Chyna Delaney was *not* in the building to see the Pinkertons? And if she was, was she a client, or an operative?

Did the Pinkertons do business with a law firm that brokered out killings for hire?

Clint decided not to wait around for Chyna to come down. After all, for whatever reason, she had taken a room in his hotel. To keep an eye on him? To meet him? And did she believe his name was Rick Hartman, or did she know him for who he was?

Well, he undoubtedly knew some things about her, now, that she didn't know he knew. They may not have been on equal footing when they met, but they certainly were now.

He went outside, hailed a cab, and told the driver to take him to his hotel.

Let Chyna Delaney make the next move.

TWENTY-SIX

When Clint got back to the hotel there was a message from Duke at the desk. It said: "Came by, found you gone. Be back at six. Be here."

Clint checked the time. It was a quarter to six.

"Were you here when this message was left?" he asked the clerk.

"Yes, sir," the man said. "The gentleman called at four."

"Will you remember him when you see him?"

"Yes, sir. I have an excellent memory."

"All right," Clint said. "I'll be at the bar. Would you send him in when he arrives?"

"Of course, sir."

"Thanks."

Clint bypassed the dining room and walked directly to the bar.

"Sir?" the bartender said.

"Beer."

Clint took his beer to a back table to await Duke's arrival at six. Given the way that coincidences were piling up on him he more than half expected Chyna Delaney to walk in on him, instead.

● ● ●

Precisely at six Duke Farrell entered, saw him, and came over to the table.

"Want a beer?" Clint asked.

"Sure."

"I'll get it."

He went to the bar and got two, brought them back, and sat down opposite his friend.

"Find out anything interesting?"

"I did," Duke said, "but I had to call in some old favors."

"Meaning?"

"Meaning that my questions may get back to somebody."

"And your name?"

"No," Duke said, "my favors will cover my name."

"Good. What did you find out?"

"Barkley, Cartwright and Lancer do, indeed, broker killings for hire."

"Which one?"

"It seems to be Richard Barkley's bailiwick," Duke said, "but my source says that everyone is in on it. It's a big moneymaker for them."

"It would be," Clint said. "Any idea who they use?"

"No," Duke said, "I couldn't get that. Also, nobody knew your man, Samuels. If he did this kind of work for them on a regular basis, he's not well-known for it."

"Anything else?"

Duke recited what he knew about the business practices of the firm. Some of it sounded shady—not as shady as murder for hire—and most of it meant nothing to Clint.

"What's Barkley look like?"

"In his fifties, the shorter of the three. They all sport full beards and dress in three-piece suits, but Barkley is the shortest and thickest built. Dark hair shot with grey. The others are older, white-haired. You can't miss him."

"Did you hear anything about the Pinkertons?"

"The Pinkertons?" Duke asked. "Like what?"

"Like do they do business?"

"I didn't hear anything specific," Duke said, "but the Pinks probably do business with most of the law firms in San Francisco."

"Have you got any favors left?"

"A few. Want me to find out about the Pinks?"

"Yes, and also about a woman whose name might or might not be Chyna Delaney." He went on to describe her to Duke.

"Since when did you need help with a woman?"

"I might need help with this one," Clint said. "She's not what she seems, and I don't even know what *that* is, yet."

"How does she fit in?"

"I don't know, but she keeps popping up in the strangest places."

"I'll see what I can get on her. The Pinkertons have been using female operatives for some time now. She might work for them."

"I thought of that," Clint said. "That's not necessarily a good thing."

"You and old Allan on good terms these days?" Duke asked.

"I don't know," Clint said. "I haven't seen him in a while. I don't think he'd be here, though. Probably Chicago or Denver."

"His health isn't good, I hear," Duke said. "His boys, Robert and William, have taken over running the agency on a day-to-day basis."

"Maybe that's why I haven't seen him in a while," Clint said. "Old Allan—he's really not that old, you know. Sixty-four or -five. He's just always been so cantankerous that he seemed old."

"Sounds like you'll miss him when he goes."

"Probably," Clint said. "He's a character, and lots of them are dying off these days."

"Amen to that," Duke said. He finished his beer and

stood up. "I'll see what I can find out about the Pinks and get back to you. Also the girl."

"I appreciate it."

"Meantime, watch your back."

"I always do."

The two men shook hands and Duke Farrell left. Clint waited for a few moments, watching the door as if willing Chyna Delaney to appear. When she didn't, he left and went into the dining room to have dinner.

TWENTY-SEVEN

Clint had the feeling there was no way he was going to get information on Chyna Delaney from Duke Farrell before he saw the woman again. He also felt that when they did meet again, the meeting would once more be instigated by her. In fact, he was going to make damn sure it was by not leaving his room. That way there would be no chance they'd run into each other accidently. If she wanted to see him, she was going to have to come looking for him.

He ate his dinner quickly and went to his room to put his plan into effect. It was a boring plan, but he couldn't think of anything to do. It was going to be even more boring if she didn't show up.

But she did.

At eight o'clock there was a knock on his door. Instinctively he knew it wasn't Duke Farrell, but since he couldn't be sure who it was he took his gun to the door.

"Who is it?"

"It's Chyna Delaney, Mr. Hartman," she said. "I've come to pay you back for this morning."

This, he thought, was going to be interesting.

He opened the door, keeping his right hand—the hand holding the gun—behind it. She was standing in the hall, her hair down instead of up, wearing something that was

107

not so conservative. It was a gown, cut very low in front to reveal some very impressive cleavage.

"Wow," he said.

"I'll take that as a compliment," she said.

"It was meant that way. Are you coming back, or going out?"

"Going out," she said. "I'm going to Portsmouth Square to gamble. I was wondering if you would like to come along. You do gamble, don't you?"

"I do," he said, "avidly, but wouldn't your escort be upset?"

She smiled and said, "I was hoping you would be my escort, silly—and my guest at a very special event."

"An event?"

She nodded and said, "A poker game, a very private one."

"You're a poker player?"

"Oh, yes," she said, "and to use your word, an avid one."

If she was working for Allan Pinkerton he might have told her of Clint's interest in poker—but Allan was ill. So maybe this young lady really was a poker player.

"What do you say?"

He had to think fast. He'd been avoiding Portsmouth Square, but now that he had the information he wanted about Richard Barkley and his law firm, maybe it was time to come out of hiding.

"I'll come with you," he said, "but there's something you should know."

"And what's that?"

"My name is not Hartman."

"It's not?"

"No."

"Then what is it?"

"It's Adams," he said, "Clint Adams."

She looked taken aback.

"I know that name."

"I thought you might. Does it make a difference to you?"

"I don't know," she said, candidly. "Why did you register under another name?"

"Because my name is known," he said, "and I didn't want to attract attention."

"You're a very famous man," she said. "I guess I can understand that."

"Too famous for your invitation?"

"Oh, no," she said, "the invitation stands, I just—well, I feel a little silly."

"Why?"

"Well, it's not as if the Gunsmith needs to be my guest to get into a private poker game in Portsmouth Square."

"Actually, I do," he said. "You see, I knew nothing about this game, and nobody knows I'm in town, so . . ."

"Well, then, how soon can you be ready?" she asked.

TWENTY-EIGHT

She waited in her room until he was ready. When she answered his knock, he was struck again by her beauty. She had a habit of taking a deep breath before each sentence, which caused her breasts to swell. He didn't know if she was doing this deliberately or not, but he didn't mind.

"Ready?" he asked.

"Yes, sir."

He put out his arm and she linked her arm through it. They went downstairs and through the lobby together that way and Clint could see he was the envy of every man they passed.

Outside they asked the doorman to get them a cab, which he did happily.

"Do you want to tell the driver where to go?" Clint asked as they got into the back of the cab.

"He knows where," she said.

The doorman closed the door and the cab started off. It was an enclosed cab, so that they were alone and had some privacy.

"Who's playing in this game tonight?" Clint asked. "There might be some people there I know."

"You'll just have to wait until we get there to find out," she said.

Too late he realized that something was wrong. First, how did the cab driver know where they were going? And second, she had her hand inside her little cloth purse.

"Chyna—"

"No more talking, Mr. Hartman."

And that was his third clue.

"I told you—"

She took her hand out of her purse and it was holding a small, two-shot derringer.

"I do not want you to speak again until I tell you to," she warned.

"I'm sorry," he said, "but you're pointing a gun at me. That doesn't inspire me to silence."

"Maybe this will."

She banged her fist on the side of the cab. He heard a panel open over his head, but before he could react the driver had reached in and clubbed him into unconsciousness. . . .

When he awoke there was screaming inside his skull. No, that wasn't it. It just hurt so much that it seemed like there was screaming inside of it.

He opened his eyes and saw Chyna sitting across from him, still holding her gun. He had no idea how long he had been out, but they were still in the cab and still moving.

He started to speak but she raised her eyebrows and pointed her gun. He decided to keep quiet until they got where they were going. If they wanted to kill him they would have, by now.

His immediate problem seemed to have nothing to do with the one that had brought him here. After all, she seemed to think he actually *was* Rick Hartman. So whatever was going on, they thought they had Rick.

Hartman had been Clint's friend for many years; and during all that time, he had lived in Labyrinth and run his saloon and gambling house, Rick's Place. Also, during all that time, Clint knew of only one occasion when Hartman had left Labyrinth, and that was to go with him on a gambling train.

He realized now that he knew little of his friend's background. He knew that the man had run some gambling establishments before, and that he had many contacts all over the country. Now he was finding out that, apparently, there was some bad blood in his past—bad blood with people who knew his name, but not what he looked like.

It was just a coincidence, then—that *horrible* word—that Clint happened to come to San Francisco on a different matter and had walked right into the middle of some trouble his friend had left behind him.

This could be fixed, he thought. *This can be explained.*

All he had to do was convince them that he was *not* Rick Hartman, and then hope that they wouldn't kill him on the spot.

Suddenly, the cab came to a stop.

"We're here," she said.

"May I speak?"

"Not yet."

The door opened and a man stuck a gun into the cab.

"When you come out you will do so slowly," the man said.

"All right."

"First hand me your gun."

Clint did so.

"Chyna comes out first, and then you."

"Naturally," Clint said. "Ladies first."

Chyna left the cab and then Clint stepped down. When he was outside both the man and the woman were holding guns on him.

"Where to now?" Clint asked.

"Follow Chyna," the man said. "I'll be right behind you."

Chyna started walking and he realized they were on a path leading to a large house. Whoever lived here was very

wealthy—rich enough to hire people to do his dirty work
for him.

"Who lives here?" he asked.

The man behind him struck him between the shoulder
blade with a fist.

"No talking."

Clint flexed his shoulders and waited. He was glad they
hadn't searched him, because he wasn't foolish enough to
come out at Chyna's request without some kind of hideout
gun. He had his little Colt New Line nestled in the small
of his back, tucked into his belt. He could have gone for it
at any time, but whether this was about him or about Rick
Hartman, he wanted to see who was behind it.

When they reached the front of the house, Chyna opened
it with a key. She either lived here or was very trusted by
whoever did.

"I'll go and get Father," she said. "Take him into the
study."

"Right. This way," the man said, using the barrel of the
gun to indicate right.

Chyna went up a wide, long flight of steps while Clint
and the driver went to the study.

"I thought for a minute you were in charge," he said
when they entered the plush, expensively furnished room.
"I guess she is."

"Shut up," the man said. "Have a seat."

Clint was getting his first good look at the man, even
better when he turned up the lamps in the room. He was
tall, slender, dark-haired, and pale, looked to be in his twen-
ties, slightly younger than Chyna, probably. And then he
had it.

"Oh, I see," he said to the man. "You're brother and
sister, aren't you?"

"Yes."

"And what's your name?"

The man didn't answer.

"Is Chyna her real name?"

No answer.

"And Delaney?" he went on. "Is that the family name?"

"That is my daughter's married name," a man's voice said.

Clint looked at the doorway and saw a man in a wheel-chair—or the wasted remains of a man. Chyna pushed the wheelchair into the room. The man in it seemed to be little but skin and bones, except for a great mane of white hair that made his face seem small.

"The family name is Sternwood," the man said.

Chyna pushed him to the center of the room. He had a plaid blanket across his lap, and his frail hands rested on it. Actually, they didn't "rest," because they shook uncontrollably.

"Charles," he said to his son, "a brandy."

"Father," Charles said, "the doctor says—"

"The doctor said I'd be dead last year," the old man cut in. "If I'm living on borrowed time I can have a brandy or two."

"All right."

As Charles walked to a sideboard filled with liquor—and liqueur—bottles, the old man said, "And one for our guest."

"Our guest?" Chyna repeated. "You call him a guest after what he's done?"

The old man laughed, a dry cackle of a laugh, and said, "He is most certainly our guest, Chyna, my dear, because he's done nothing to us."

"But, Father," Chyna said, with a look that turned her beautiful face ugly, "he's Rick Hartman."

"No, my dear," the old man said, "he most certainly is not. His name is Clint Adams, although many know him as the Gunsmith."

TWENTY-NINE

"I tried to tell her that," Clint said.

"He's lying," Chyna said. "Why would he register as Rick Hartman?"

"Well," Sternwood said, "that's something we'd have to ask Mr. Adams, isn't it?"

Charles, somewhat puzzled by what was going on, handed Clint his glass of brandy, and then took one to his father.

"By the way, sir," Sternwood said, "my name is General Arthur Sternwood, at your service."

"General Sternwood?" Clint repeated, recognizing the name. He'd never met the man but knew he was in the presence of a great soldier. "I'm honored to meet you, General."

"Well, you're very kind to an old man," Sternwood said, "but perhaps you could answer my daughter's question?"

"Well, sir," Clint said, "I'm in San Francisco on some business and didn't want anyone to know I was here, so I registered under an assumed name."

"But why that name?" Sternwood asked.

"It was the only one I could think of at the time," Clint said.

"Oh, so it was just a coincidence that you picked the name of the man who killed my sister?" Chyna said angrily.

Clint sat there, stunned. He appreciated the fact that they had stunned him, for it kept him from explaining further that Rick Hartman was actually a friend of his. Now he was glad he hadn't mentioned it.

"Killed your sister?"

"Chyna," Sternwood said, "I think you should let Mr. Adams and I talk awhile . . . alone."

"Father—" she began.

"I don't think—" Charles started.

"I am going to have to do some talking, I'm afraid, to keep Mr. Adams from filing kidnapping charges against the two of you."

"And assault," Clint said, touching the bump on his head.

"Assault?" Sternwood asked, giving both of his children a long look.

"Chyna had me club him on the head to keep him quiet," Charles said. "I didn't hit him that hard."

"I think you both should leave."

"At least take this," Chyna said, offering her father her derringer.

"That's silly," Sternwood said, waving the weapon away. "I'm in no danger from Mr. Adams."

"Not while I have his gun," Charles said proudly.

"You missed one, son," Clint said, producing the New Line from behind his back.

Charles looked crestfallen.

"Charles, give Mr. Adams back his gun and then I insist you both leave! Now!"

Charles gave Clint his weapon back, and then he and Chyna left, grudgingly.

"I'm truly sorry about this, sir," Sternwood said. "It was a simple case of mistaken identity. I hope you won't press charges against either of my children."

"They're not children, General," Clint said, tucking both his guns away, "but no, I don't intend to press charges."

"Excellent!" Sternwood said. "Let's drink to it, then."

They both sipped their brandy and the old man immediately began to cough. His pallor became even paler—if that were possible—and Clint left the chair he was in to attend to the old man. He got down on one knee next to the wheelchair and waited.

"Is there anything I can do?" he asked solicitously, when the coughing stopped.

"Water," the old man croaked. "The decanter by the brandy."

Clint went to the sideboard, poured a glass of water and brought it to General Sternwood. The old man sipped the water, and that seemed to ease his distress.

"You're very kind," he said, handing the water back. "Especially in light of what's happened."

"No harm done, really," Clint said, returning the glass to the sideboard. Then he felt his head and added, "No permanent damage, anyway."

"Tell me, sir," Sternwood said, his voice stronger, "do you always wear two guns?"

"Not always, no," Clint said. "Just when I feel I need a backup."

"And you felt that tonight, when my daughter invited you out?"

"Yes, sir."

"Why is that?"

"Because I knew something wasn't right."

"And how did you know that?" Sternwood asked. "I'm given to understand that my daughter has a certain . . . way about her."

"She does," Clint said. "She most certainly does."

"Then why were you suspicious?" Sternwood asked. "Was it the way she approached you this morning?"

"Maybe," Clint said, "but I've been approached by strange women before."

"Yes," Sternwood said, "I had heard that about you. What, then, uh, tipped you off?"

"I saw her on Market Street earlier."

"And what was she doing?"

"Well . . . she was leaving a building I was watching."

"What building?"

"I don't know the address," Clint said, "but it has a law firm in it, Barkley, Cartwright and Lancer."

Sternwood made a face.

"Do you have some business with that firm of . . . reprobates?"

"I do."

"I'm sorry to hear that," Sternwood said.

"You see," Clint explained, "someone's been trying to kill me for about two months and, as I understand it, they were hired through that law firm."

"That does not surprise me. Did you think my daughter was involved?"

"It was a little too much of a coincidence for me."

"Well, sir, I'm afraid it was a coincidence. You see, we—my family, that is—maintains an office there to see to our business."

"Ah," Clint said. He hadn't gone inside, so he hadn't found that out.

"And was that all?"

"No," Clint said. "I followed her after that."

"Ah, where to?"

"Another building on Market Street."

"And who was in that building?"

"Well, among other businesses and firms, the Pinkertons."

"Oh, I see," Sternwood said.

"Do you have business with the Pinkertons, General?"

"Actually, we do, and we have for some time, on the same matter."

"The murder of your daughter?"

"Yes."

"Trying to find the man who did it?"

"Yes, indeed."

"And that man would be . . . ?"

"The man we suspected you of being," Sternwood said. "Rick Hartman."

THIRTY

"When did this happen?"

"It was ten years ago," Sternwood said. "Carmen was my oldest daughter. Five older than Chyna, eight years the senior of Charles."

"So they were children when she was killed?"

"Not quite," the old man said. "Chyna had just turned nineteen, and I believe Charles was sixteen. They were devastated by the brutal murder of their older sister."

"How did it happen?"

"She was strangled, and sexually assaulted," Sternwood said.

"And how do you know it was this Rick Hartman?"

"She was seeing Hartman at the time," Sternwood said. "She was in love with him, but he was a gambler and a womanizer. I warned her about him."

"So when she was found dead you assumed it was him?" Clint asked.

"He was never seen again after that day," Sternwood said. "Why would he disappear like that if he didn't kill her?"

"And you've been looking for him ever since?"

"Yes, sir," Sternwood said, "and we thought we had found him today."

"I'm sorry to disappoint you. When did you hire the Pinkertons to look for him?"

"Eight years ago," Sternwood replied.

"When the trail was two years cold?"

"My wife died eight years ago," Sternwood said. "I promised her on her deathbed that I would find the man who killed our Carmen. The day after her funeral I went to see Allan Pinkerton, who swore he would not rest until he found Rick Hartman."

"You know Allan personally?"

"For many years—and you do, as well?"

"Yes, but probably not as long. I've heard he's ill."

"He's dying," Sternwood said, "which is something he and I have in common, I'm afraid. How old would you say I look?"

Clint didn't answer.

"Never mind, that was rude. I look eighty but in reality I'm several years younger than Allan."

Clint agreed with the old man. He did look eighty or older.

"Can I ask you a question, sir?"

"Of course," Sternwood said. "The least I can do for your trouble is answer your questions."

"How did you know that someone by the name of Rick Hartman had registered at my hotel?"

"We have people in some of the hotels in the city, and where we don't the Pinkertons do. We—or they—are to be notified whenever someone by that name checks into a hotel."

"And who was notified about me?"

"The Pinkertons, and they in turn told my daughter, Chyna. They have been dealing with her for the past few years, since I ended up in this confounded chair."

"And Chyna took it upon herself to get a room there and check me out?"

"She did."

"That's a brave and foolish thing to do."

"I know," Sternwood said. "I forbade her to do it, but she doesn't listen to me. She never did. She's a headstrong girl."

"And beautiful," Clint said.

"Yes," Sternwood said, "yes."

"I'm extremely sorry that I picked that name out of a hat to register under."

"Oh," Sternwood said, "but you didn't, did you?"

"Sir?"

"That would be one coincidence too many, wouldn't it?" Sternwood asked.

"Sir, I—"

"Sir!" Sternwood said, with some steel to his tone. "I believe you chose the name because you have a friend with the same name. Isn't that true?"

"General Sternwood—" Clint tried again.

Sternwood waved a hand and said, "Never mind, never mind. You don't strike me as a man who would give up a friend."

Clint didn't answer. Suddenly, the old man seemed to deflate and, if possible, shrink further into his chair.

"I'm afraid I've had enough for today," he said, his tone now thin and weak. "I'll have Charles take you back to your hotel."

"I'll find him."

"There's no need," Sternwood said, and, as if on cue, Charles and Chyna walked in. Somehow, the old man had signaled them.

"Take Mr. Adams back to his hotel, Charles," Sternwood said.

"I'll do it, Charles," Chyna said. "You take Father back to his room."

"Chyna—" Sternwood said, but he didn't have the strength to finish.

"Charles," she said, "you can get him up the stairs better than I can."

"But, Chyna—"

"Just do it!" she snapped. She turned to Clint and said sweetly to him, "Mr. Adams? I'll take you back to your hotel now."

THIRTY-ONE

Chyna took Clint back to his hotel in a buggy, not in the cab that had brought them to her father's house.

"You father is quite a man," Clint said.

She looked at him quickly, as if she were going to make a sharp retort, but she paused a moment and then spoke in a surprisingly gentle voice.

"Yes, he is," she said. "He's a great man, as well. That's why it eats away at him that he hasn't brought to justice the man who killed Carmen."

"It only eats away at him?"

"At all of us."

They rode in silence for a while, with Chyna driving the buggy, before she spoke again.

"I suppose I owe you an apology."

"I suppose you do."

He waited a moment and when one was not forthcoming he asked, "Was that it?"

"All right," she said, tight-lipped, "I apologize."

"Apology accepted."

"Can I ask you a question?"

"Sure."

"Why did you bring that extra gun?"

"I thought I'd need it," Clint replied.

"Against me?"

"Yes."

"Why didn't you use it?"

"I didn't feel I had to."

"Even when I was pointing my gun at you?"

"I didn't think you'd shoot me."

"I wouldn't have," she said, and then added, "At least, not until after you talked to my father."

"You're not a killer, Chyna."

"Maybe not," she said, "but I could kill the man who murdered my sister."

"Rick Hartman?"

"Yes."

"Are you sure he did it?"

"Who else could it have been?"

"Was your sister seeing any other men?"

"No," she said bitterly, "but he was seeing other women. That's the kind of man he was, only she refused to see it."

"You saw it, though?"

"Yes."

"Even at nineteen?"

"At nineteen," she said, slowly, "I knew a lot more about men than my sister did."

Clint decided to accept that remark without asking her to explain it.

She pulled the buggy to a stop in front of the hotel and waved the doorman away as he started forward.

"Are you coming in?" he asked.

"I'll be going home."

"Checking out of the hotel?"

"I was never really checked in," she said. "I was just . . . using one of their rooms."

"I see," Clint said, getting down from the buggy.

"You're not going to go to the police?"

"No," he said.

"Not even after my brother hit you?"

"Like he said," Clint answered, "he didn't hit me all that hard."

"I suppose I should thank you for that, too."

"I wouldn't want to put you out," Clint said. "Chyna?"

"Yes?"

"Was your sister seeing anyone before Rick Hartman?"

"Yes."

"And did she break up with him because of, uh, Hartman?"

"Yes."

"Was he angry?"

"If you think Wesley Dawson killed Carmen you can forget it. Wes loved her."

"You know him?"

"He's from one of the finest families in San Francisco. She should have married him."

"Is he still in San Francisco?" Clint asked.

"Yes."

"And do you see him?"

"If it's any of your business," she said, "I'm engaged to him."

THIRTY-TWO

Clint stopped for a beer before he went up to his room. He had a lot to think about.

First, with the landslide of coincidence that was going on around him, could General Sternwood and his son and daughter be talking about another Rick Hartman? And if they *were* talking about the Rick he knew, who's to say that he wasn't a different man ten years ago?

Clint didn't believe for a moment that Rick Hartman could kill a woman—certainly not the way Carmen Sternwood had been killed. He did, however, believe that the *Sternwoods* believed Rick was guilty. The only way to be sure of what happened was to ask Rick, but Clint couldn't do that until he returned to Labyrinth. There was just too much to be said to be able to do it by telegram. At least now he knew why Rick hardly ever left Labyrinth? What he didn't know was why the Pinkertons had not found him in eight years. Old Allan usually employed some pretty competent people—and, of course, some incompetent people. Maybe Allan was appeasing his old friend the general, and had simply never put his best people on the case.

So what was he to do now? He still had his own problems to contend with, but what about Rick Hartman? Did he even know that the Sternwoods in San Francisco wanted

him for murder? What should he do? Forget about con-
fronting Richard Barkley or try to investigate a ten-year-
old murder in the hopes of clearing his friend?

While he was finishing the dregs of his beer he looked
up and saw Duke Farrell come into the hotel bar. Duke saw
him, and hurried over and sat down.

"I found out about that woman you asked after," he
said.

"She's General Sternwood's daughter."

Duke sat back and gave Clint a disgusted look.

"If you know this stuff, why am I wasting my time?"
he asked.

"I only found out tonight," Clint said, and told Duke
how.

"Wait a minute," Duke said. "I know Rick Hartman.
He wouldn't kill a woman the way Carmen Sternwood was
killed."

"Were you here then?" Clint asked.

"No," Duke said, "I didn't move here until later, but
everyone in San Francisco knows about the Sternwood
murder. I didn't know that the family was blaming it on
Rick Hartman. Does he know?"

"I don't know," Clint said, "and I don't want to chance
sending him a telegram. Sternwood suspects that I know
him. If he tracked Rick down through my telegram, I'd
never forgive myself."

"I don't blame you. What are you gonna do? You still
have your problem to figure out."

"I know," Clint said. "I can go and see Barkley tomorrow. Maybe I can scare him into giving up the name
of whoever hired him."

"And if you can't?"

"I may have to drop it for a while and look into Carmen
Sternwood's murder."

"Ten years after the fact?"

"There was another man," Clint said. "She dropped him
because of Rick."

"Who?"

"A man named Wesley Dawson."

"The Dawson family?" Duke whistled soundlessly.

"You know them?" Clint asked.

"They're almost as rich and respected as the Stern-woods. Wait a minute. Isn't the daughter, Chyna, engaged to him?"

"That's right."

"And he was in love with her sister?"

"Right again. What do you know about Wesley Daw-son?"

"I know he'd be more inclined to kill a woman than Rick Hartman would."

"Why do you say that?"

"Because I've seen him beat a woman in public," Duke said. "It was in Portsmouth Square . . . the Alhambra, I think. He lost his temper one night and had to be pulled off of her."

"Who was she?"

"I don't recall, but I know she went there with him," Duke said.

"He escorts a woman to a casino and then beats her up in public? Not a smart man."

"He gambles a lot, loses a *lot*, and then loses his temper."

"Sounds like a suspect to me," Clint said. "What would a smart lady like Chyna Delaney want with him, though?"

"It's a good marriage for both families."

"An arranged marriage?"

"Not exactly arranged," Duke said, "maybe just . . . agreed upon."

"Well," Clint said, "I guess I'll add Wesley Dawson to my list of people to see tomorrow."

"First the lawyer?"

"First the lawyer," Clint said.

"Want some backup?" Duke asked.

"Thanks, but I think I can handle this, Duke," Clint said.

Duke was a friend, and was smart in many ways, but Clint didn't know if he could trust the man to watch his back. He didn't know what Duke could do with a gun.

"All right, then," Duke said. "Watch your own back and let me know what happens."

"I will."

Duke left. Clint debated whether or not to have another beer, then decided against it and went to bed. He had a big day tomorrow.

THIRTY-THREE

Clint woke the next morning ready to confront the lawyer, Richard Barkley. What he didn't want to do, however, was call on Barkley in his own office. He needed to isolate him, get him someplace neutral.

He had breakfast in the hotel dining room while he considered his options. When he finally had a plan, he left the hotel, got a cab, and took it to Market Street.

His plan was simple. Locate himself in the same doorway as yesterday, only this time he'd wait for Barkley to come out. He had the man's description from Duke: short, thick-set, bearded. He stayed in that doorway all day, and by the time the man finally appeared—around five o'clock—he was in a bad mood. He'd hoped Barkley would at least come out for lunch, but he hadn't. By the time he did appear Clint was ravenous.

Which was too bad for Barkley.

Barkley came out of the building a little after five. He seemed to be the partner who adhered more rigidly to the banker's hour workday. Clint was hoping he wouldn't immediately hail a cab. There was no way he could have had one waiting, and he didn't know where the man lived. If

135

Barkley did grab a cab, Clint's mood was only going to worsen.

Luckily, the man decided to walk. Maybe he had a club or saloon he stopped in after work. Whatever the reason it was enough for Clint that he was on foot. He did the same thing he'd done with Chyna the day before, remained on his side of the street as he followed the lawyer.

As he had hoped, the man stopped in a saloon, probably for an after-work drink. He didn't know if there was a wife waiting for him at home, but if there was she was going to have to wait a little longer for her husband to come home for dinner.

A saloon was as good a place as any to brace the man.

Richard Barkley settled down at a table with his post-work, pre-going home drink. He usually needed a good whiskey or two before going home to his wife of twenty-two years who, for a good half of them—the last half, not the first—had become the perfect example of a shrew. He had a mistress nicely tucked away, but this was not his day to see her, so on days like this he made do with whiskey.

He didn't see the man approaching his table until it was too late.

"This is a private table," he said, as the man sat down across from him with a beer.

"I know that," the man said. "That's why I'm sitting here."

"I don't understand," Barkley said.

"We have some business, Mr. Barkley."

"Do I know you?"

"Well," Clint said, "I think you know of me. My name is Clint Adams."

Barkley rose up in his seat in surprise, then settled back down and tried to brazen it out.

"I don't believe I do know you—"

Clint took out the letter Barkley had written to Samuels and put it on the table.

"You ought to be careful what you put in print, Mr. Barkley," he said. "As a lawyer, I'd think you'd already know that."

"Are you going to kill me?" the lawyer asked.

"If I was going to do that," Clint said, "you would never have made it three feet out the door of your building."

"What do you want, then?"

"I want to know who wants me dead."

Barkley seemed in his element now that he knew he wasn't going to die.

"I would imagine a lot of people would like you dead," he said. "I'd think you'd know that without me telling you."

"Touché," Clint said, "but let's stop fencing, Mr. Barkley, shall we? I could always change my mind about killing you."

"And what would that accomplish?" the lawyer asked. "It wouldn't help you find out who wants you dead, would it?"

"I could just give up on you," Clint said, "and ask your partners."

"They wouldn't know," Barkley said. "I handle that end of the business."

"Well, then," Clint said, "maybe I could do it just for my own personal satisfaction."

Barkley looked into Clint's eyes and said, "Okay, wait."

"For what?"

"I have to think."

"I hope you're thinking about the name."

"If I give you a name," Barkley said, "I could end up dead."

"You could end up that way if you don't," Clint pointed out.

"Then where's my choice?"

Clint leaned forward and showed the lawyer the Colt New Line he was holding in his hand.

"One would be sooner, and one later."

Nervously Barkley said, "You couldn't shoot me in here."

"This is a nice quiet saloon, Barkley, filled with lawyers and businessmen, am I right?"

Barkley didn't answer.

"Do you see anyone in here who would stop me from walking out after I shot you?"

"You've got to give me a chance—"

"To do what? Think some more? Think of a way out? Or a lie? Sorry, lawyer," Clint said, cocking the hammer on the gun, "your time is up."

"Wait!" Barkley whispered harshly. "For God's sake . . . I'll give you a name."

"Not just a name," Clint said. "It has to be the *right* name."

"I can give you the name of the man who contacted me," Barkley said, "the man who pays me, but I can't give you the name of the man he works for."

"Can't," Clint asked, "or won't?"

"Can't," Barkley said, "because I don't know it."

"Then I guess I'll have to make do with the name you do know."

Barkley nervously finished his whiskey, looked around to make sure no one could hear, and gave Clint the name.

THIRTY-FOUR

"I don't know him," Duke Farrell said.

"I don't, either," Clint said, "so what's he doing putting a price on my head?"

They were in Duke's office at Duke's hotel, just the two of them sitting on either side of his desk.

"Does this mean we're not meeting in secret anymore?" Duke asked when Clint appeared at his door.

"It means I have a question I need answered right away," Clint had answered.

The question was: "Who is Henry Enright?"

To which Duke answered, "I don't know him. What did Barkley tell you about him?"

"That he came into his office, put cash on his desk, and said there would be more where that came from once I was dead," Clint said.

"Specifically you?"

"Who else?"

"No, I mean did he say 'Clint Adams,' or 'The Gunsmith?' "

"I don't know," Clint said. "Why do you think that's important?"

"I'm just trying to get a clear picture here," Duke said.

"Does this man—or whoever he works for—want the legend dead, or the man?"

"I see what you mean now," Clint said, getting up from his chair. "It's good question. I'll ask him when I find him."

"Where are you going to look?"

"Denver."

"What?" Duke said with a puzzled frown as Clint left his office.

Clint had decided to send a telegram to his friend Talbot Roper in Denver. Roper was a private detective who had once worked for the Pinkertons but who had long since gone out on his own, establishing himself as the best in the business. He had connections in most major cities in the country. Maybe he knew, or could find out, who or what a Henry Enright was.

Once he sent the telegram and left his hotel address for the reply to be delivered, Clint got another idea. There was a detective agency right here in town who might be able to help him.

The Pinkertons.

Clint didn't know who was running this office of the Pinkertons. There was no love lost between himself or either Robert or William, but he believed he would be able to talk with Robert.

He went to Market Street, to the offices of the Pinkerton Agency there, and presented himself at the front desk. Behind the middle-aged receptionist, on the wall, was the logo: the eye who never sleeps. It was one of the few good ideas Clint thought Allan Pinkerton had ever had.

"Yes?"

"I'd like to see a Pinkerton," he said.

"A detective?" she asked. "Or an actual Pinkerton family member?"

"Is there a Pinkerton family member here?" he asked.

"No, sir. William is in Chicago, and Robert is in New York. And *Mister* Pinkerton—"

"I know about Allan Pinkerton's illness," Clint said. That would explain why William was in Chicago. "Who is in charge of this office, then?"

"That would be our Mr. Morgan, sir, James Morgan."

"All right," he said, "I'll speak to your Mr. Morgan, then."

"Who may I say is calling, sir?"

"Clint Adams."

"And will he know what it's in reference to?" she asked.

"He'll react to my name, I think," Clint said. If the man didn't, then he'd figure he was in the wrong place.

"Yes, sir," she said, rising from her chair. "I'll tell him. Please wait here."

She went through a door, closing it firmly behind her, and then reappeared several minutes later.

"Will you follow me, sir?"

"Of course."

Now he was allowed to go through that door and follow her down a corridor to a door that had JAMES MORGAN, VICE PRESIDENT written on it. She knocked, opened it, and said to Clint, "You may go in."

"Thank you."

As he entered, a bearded, bespectacled man in his early forties rose from his desk and hurried toward him with his hand outstretched.

"My dear fellow," James Morgan said, "how nice to meet you. Of course when Annie told me who was waiting in reception—well, you could have knocked me over with a feather."

"Well," Clint said, taken aback by the welcome he was receiving, "it's very nice to meet you, too."

"Come, sit down, sit down," Morgan said, leading Clint to a leather visitor's chair. "May I get you something? A drink? Some coffee? A cigar?"

"No, nothing, thanks," Clint said. "I'm quite comfortable."

"Very well," Morgan said, moving around behind his desk and seating himself. "Please, tell me what I can do for you."

"Well, maybe you can start by telling me how Allan is doing?"

"Yes, well, I'm quite aware of your, ah, history with Mr. Pinkerton."

"Are you?"

"Oh, yes," Morgan said, "the family keeps its vice president quite well informed."

"That's good to know."

"In any case, Mr. Pinkerton's condition is tragic. He's quite ill, you see, very possibly dying."

"I'm sorry to hear that," Clint said. "Despite all our differences, I respect Allan."

"Yes, well, I'm sure he returns the sentiment. But then, you didn't come here simply to inquire as to Mr. Pinkerton's health, did you?"

"No," Clint said. "I have a problem you might be able to help me with. At least, I hope you will."

"And what would that be?"

"Someone is trying to kill me."

"You'll forgive me for asking, sir," Morgan said, "but . . . is that an unusual occurrence for you?"

"Unfortunately, it's not," Clint said, "but this is different. You see, someone from San Francisco has put a price on my head."

"Oh, dear," Morgan said, "that would be distressing, wouldn't it?"

"Very much so," Clint said.

"So you would like us to find out who it is?"

"Not quite," Clint said. "See, I know the price was brokered by Richard Barkley of Barkley, Cartwright and Lancer."

"A disreputable firm, at best," Morgan said. "We know them quite well."

"I would think you would. Well, I've gotten a name from Mr. Barkley."

"Really?" Morgan looked surprised. "How did you manage that?"

"I used a little persuasion."

"Ah," Morgan said, as if he knew the type of persuasion Clint was capable of. "And what was the name?"

"Enright," Clint said. "Henry Enright."

"Enright, Enright," Morgan repeated, frowning. "I don't believe I know the name."

Clint stared at the man and knew, instinctively, that he was lying. He wondered why.

THIRTY-FIVE

"Enright . . ." Morgan said again—more than one time too many.

"Maybe you could find out for me?"

Morgan smiled, a very professional smile.

"We could certainly try, sir."

"Now, for your fee—"

"Oh, no, sir," Morgan said, "I'm sure Mr. Pinkerton would not want us to bill you. Professional courtesy, and all that."

"But I'm not a private detective."

"A minor technicality," Morgan said, "one that I, as vice president of operations for this office, can arrange to overlook. May I ask where you're staying?"

Clint told him.

"Very good. I'm sure we can have some information on that name for you in a few days. I can have one of our operatives come to your hotel with the information."

"That would be very helpful."

"Not at all, sir, not at all."

There was an awkward silence then, and Clint realized that he was supposed to leave.

"I'll be going then," he said, standing up.

Morgan walked him to the door and shook his hand

firmly—too firmly, Clint thought, as if he was trying to convince Clint of his sincerity.

"We'll get back to you as soon as we can. You can just go back down the hall the way you came to get out."

"I'll find it," Clint said. "Thank you for your time."

Clint retraced his steps as the door closed behind him, and found himself in the reception area once again with Annie.

"So that's your Mr. Morgan," he said.

"Well," she said, "not my Mr. Morgan."

"Of course not," Clint said. "I can see that you have much too much class for him."

She smiled and patted her hair, which was tightly wrapped in a bun at the back of her head. Clint took a better look at her. She appeared to be in her forties, and if she took her hair down and applied a little color to her face he realized she'd be quite pretty.

"Besides," Clint said, "he's probably married."

"Actually," she said, "he's not. I don't think—" she started, then slapped her hand over her mouth.

"You don't think any woman would have him?" Clint asked. "He is a bit pompous, isn't he?"

"I shouldn't say," she replied. "After all, he is my boss." But she was grinning and on the verge of laughing out loud.

"What's your name?" he asked.

"Ann Bennett," she said. "Annie, everyone calls me."

"Mrs. Bennett?"

"Miss."

"Miss Bennett," Clint said, taking her hand, "I hope to get to see you again, soon."

"Well," she said, "how nice."

"Good day."

"Good day to you, too, Mr. Adams."

Clint left the office and started down the hall. He still thought Morgan was lying to him, but was he getting paranoid? Was he starting to think that everyone was keeping something from him? That everyone was involved in this plot to kill him?

Clint knew men who'd lived a long time with reputations, who'd eventually begun to see plots and assassins behind every tree. He hoped that that was not what was happening to him. James Morgan simply had the look of a liar when Clint asked him about Enright.

Before he left the floor, and the building, he thought of something and went back.

"Did you forget something?" Ann Bennett asked, a bit hopefully.

"I'm sorry, but Mr. Morgan said he was going to have an operative call at my hotel, and I can't recall the name."

"Oh, dear," she said. "I can ask him—"

"No," Clint said, "maybe you could just tell me—I think it started with an 'N'. No, that's not it. It was En . . . something."

"Enright?" she prompted.

Clint felt a rush of satisfaction.

"That was it, Enright . . . I can't remember the first name . . ."

"Henry Enright," she said. "He's one of our very best operatives."

"Really? Well, that makes me feel a lot better, then. Thank you, Miss Bennett."

"Please," she said, "call me Annie."

"And when we meet again," he said, "you'll have to call me Clint."

"That would be . . . nice," she said.

He knew she was waiting for him to ask where or when they could meet again, but at the moment he had something else on his mind. He hated to disappoint her, but maybe he could make it up to her later. He really would like to see her with her hair down.

"Good day, Annie," he said again, and left her looking disappointed.

A Pinkerton, he thought on the way out of the building.
The price on his head had been placed there by a damned
Pinkerton.

But for whom?

THIRTY-SIX

When Clint got to his hotel there was a reply from Talbot Roper waiting for him. It said, very simply: "ENRIGHT PINKERTON OP. BEWARE," and was signed, "TAL ROPER."

Well, it was nice to get some validation from Roper on this. He was dead right about Morgan lying to him about not knowing Enright. But what exactly did "Beware" mean? Was it general, or specifically referring to Enright?

Clint was standing off to the side of the desk, trying to decide whether or not to send another telegram to Roper, when Chyna Delaney walked into the lobby. He watched her as she scanned the lobby for a moment while the men in the lobby—himself included—scanned her. The dress she was wearing was slightly less than modest, revealing not a lot of cleavage, but enough to make other women hate her on the spot. Somehow, Clint didn't think this concerned Chyna Delaney at all.

Finally, her eyes fell on him and she started toward him.

"Mr. Adams."

"Mrs. Delaney," he said. "Is there something I can help you with?"

"I would like to talk to you," she said, then looked around and added, "In private."

"Would my room be private enough?"

She hesitated.

"Or would that damage your reputation?"

She lifted her chin and said, "Your room would be fine."

"Then follow me," he said.

He went up the stairs ahead of her, listened to her skirts rustling behind him. He imagined she was fuming at having to walk behind him.

He led her to his room, unlocked the door, and allowed her to precede him. The bed was unmade. She walked to it, seemed to consider whether to sit on it or not, then decided against it.

"Perhaps the chair," he said, indicating the wooden chair by the window.

"I can stand, thank you."

"Suit yourself," he said. "Would you like me to close the door?"

"I am not a child, Mr. Adams," she said. "Close it or leave it open, as you prefer."

"I prefer it closed," he said, and closed it with a slam. The sound made her jump; she tried to cover it, but there was no denying she was nervous. He just didn't know why.

"All right, Mrs. Delaney," Clint said. "What's on your mind?"

She paced back and forth a bit, rubbing her hands together before answering.

"I'm not sure."

"What?"

"I'm not sure why I came here," she said angrily.

"Well, if you don't know, I sure don't," he said. "Maybe you want to pull a gun on me again?"

"No."

"Club me over the head?"

"No."

"Apologize to me again?"

She whirled on him angrily and he waited for her sharp

tongue to heap venom on him, but then she surprised him.

"Yes," she said, "yes, that's it." She closed the distance between them, pulled his head down to her, and kissed him. As she did so, she rubbed her body against him, grinding herself into him until his body had no choice but to respond.

"Yes," she said again, pulling her head back, her eyes glistening, "I came here to apologize to you . . . for a long, long time . . ."

THIRTY-SEVEN

Clint found Chyna's energy—and her body—amazing.

He undressed her and was surprised to find that her breasts were not as large as they seemed when she was clothed, but they were remarkably firm, as was the rest of her body. There was not an inch of her that was a disappointment.

He laid her on the bed, undressed, and joined her there. She reached for him, held him tightly, and commenced with her apologies.

He explored her body first, using his hands and his mouth on her until she was gasping. He was nestled between her legs, avidly tasting her, and she groped for him, imploring him to never stop. Stop he did, though, but only to mount her and drive himself into her. He cupped her solid buttocks and began to just slam into her as hard as he could. She gasped and cried out, but she was a big, solid girl and she could take it. In fact, she gave as good as she got, driving up to meet each of his thrusts. They went at each other that way for some time, and the air around them filled with the sounds and scents of their exertions.

"Top," Chyna said, eventually, "I want to be on top . . ."

She broke their coupling apart just long enough to switch

positions, and then she took him back inside of her and began to ride him hard. He palmed her breasts, brought them to his mouth and sucked her nipples until they were as hard as little diamonds. She bit her lip each time she came down on him, grunting with the effort, grinding on him for a moment before raising up again. She was so wet, and was bouncing around on him so hard, that a couple of times he slid free of her. She groaned her dismay each time and gathered him back in. Finally, they were both so close they could feel it, each of them trembling as their passion threatened to explode . . . and then did. . . .

"That was some apology," he said.

"Mmmm," she said, pressing tightly again him, "and I'm not finished yet."

"You mean I deserve more?"

"I told you," Chyna said, her hands snaking down between his legs, "I intend to apologize for a long, long time."

"We're talking tonight, though, right," he said, "not years?"

"Tonight will be enough," she promised. "By morning, I don't think either one of us is going to be able to walk."

"I don't think I could walk now," he said.

She straddled him, feeling him start to stiffen beneath her, and said, "Well, then, by morning you'll probably just be able to crawl."

Later, he turned her over onto her belly so he could kiss her back and massage her buttocks. He slid his tongue down that beautiful line that all women have, that line that runs down the center of their back and disappears between their buttocks.

"Mmm," she said, as he worked on her with his tongue and his lips, "no man has ever kissed me . . . there . . . before . . . oooh . . ."

"Then they don't know what they've been missing," he said, "and I do . . ."

Still later, while she was on her stomach, he slid his hand beneath her and probed her with his finger, getting her nice and wet. Then he straddled her, slid his stiffened penis between her thighs and up into her. She gasped and lifted her hips. He grabbed one of the pillows and put it beneath her, then supported his weight on his arms and took her that way, in long, slow strokes. His tempo increased little by little, going faster and faster until finally he was ramming himself into her from behind, mindless for once of anything but his own pleasure. When he exploded into her, he bellowed like an animal and then became aware, in the silence that followed, that she was laughing uncontrollably.

"I wasn't laughing *at* you," she said, giggling. "Well, maybe I was. I mean, you sounded like a *bull*!"

"You could give a man a problem laughing at him, you know," he said. "We're fragile creatures of ego, you know."

"Oh, yeah," she said, "right, I know. Why is it, Clint, that a man with your reputation seems to have no ego at all?"

"Are we talking about me," he asked, "or a man *like* me?"

She was sitting in the center of the bed, legs folded, gloriously bare-breasted. He decided that she looked so large-breasted when dressed because she was thicker in the upper torso than most women he'd known. Not unattractively so, because it was part of what made her so wonderfully firm, but when dressed it just looked like . . . well, breasts.

She saw him studying her and suddenly crossed her arms over herself.

"I know," she said. "I look . . . fuller when I'm dressed."

"You look lovely," he said, "dressed or undressed."

"I'm just built slightly weird," she said. "It drives the dressmakers crazy."

"Well," he said, reaching for her and pulling her close, "that gives me something in common with your dressmakers, doesn't it?"

She climbed aboard him, straddling him, and they kissed and explored each other with their hands. She felt how hard he was, he felt how wet she was, and with just a little bit of movement he was suddenly nestled tightly up inside of her. They began to rock together that way, more tightly pressed together than at any time during that night, actually intertwined, arms and legs and other parts, so that they almost seemed, in the semidarkness of the room, to be one single creature rather than two people who were thoroughly enjoying themselves . . . and each other. . . .

THIRTY-EIGHT

By morning, they were both so hungry they decided to chance walking. They made it to the hotel dining room, where they each devoured a breakfast of steak and eggs.

"Can I ask you something, Chyna?" he said, during a shared second pot of coffee.

"Do I have any secrets left?" she asked. "You now know what drives my dressmakers crazy about me. Go ahead, ask your question."

"It's about the Pinkertons."

"Oh."

"Do you know a man named Enright?"

"Enright? Is he a Pinkerton?"

"Yes."

She frowned, thought a moment, then shook her head.

"No, I don't."

"Who do you talk to when you go to their offices?" he asked.

"That idiot, Morgan."

"Why do you call him an idiot?"

"Because he's always trying to...to placate me. He calls me 'little lady.' I can't stand him."

"Why not send your brother up there?"

"My brother, while I love him, is something of a milksop," she said.

"He handled me all right, the other night."

"He hit you from behind, Clint," she reminded him. "That's not handling you."

"After all these years," he said, getting back to the Pinkertons, "why do you keep paying them?"

"They're the best," she said. "They can't seem to find my sister's killer, but they're still the best. My father insists on employing them."

"But do you really expect to find the killer after all this time?"

She hesitated before answering.

"Expect to? No. But we still have hopes," she said. "My father still has hopes."

"Forgive me, but . . . what about your fiancé?"

"What about him?"

"Well . . . if you're getting married, why are you here with me?"

"I told you," she said. "I owed you an apology. Besides, once I'm married I won't be getting the kind of . . . treatment I got from you last night. Wesley is not . . . capable of that kind of passion."

"Then why marry him?"

"Joining our families will make us a powerful force in San Francisco—possibly the most powerful force."

"You mean it will make your father and his father powerful," he said. "What about you? What about love?"

"I don't believe in love," she said.

"Why not?" he asked, then kicked himself because he immediately knew what the answer would be.

"Love got my sister killed."

What kind of an argument could he present in the face of that?

After breakfast, she said she had to go home.

"I have to change my clothes, and then I have . . . well, business to take care of."

He walked her out to the front of the hotel and waited while the doorman got her a cab.

"Clint?

"Yes."

She turned to him, but didn't touch him.

"Last night was wonderful."

"Yes, it was."

"But it can never happen again. Do you understand that?"

"Perfectly."

"I knew you would, you bastard," she said, and got into her cab.

THIRTY-NINE

Clint decided to make another visit to Market Street, this time to the Pinkerton offices. Mr. James Morgan had some explaining to do.

On his way there, Clint made his final decision to force the issue—both issues—today. First, he had to find this Enright and get the name of the person who had put the price on his head.

After that, he was going to talk to Mr. Wesley Dawson, because he was dead sure that, even ten years ago, Rick Hartman could not have murdered a woman. That left Dawson as the only suspect. After all, she *had* dumped him to go to Rick. Of course, Clint had no way of knowing if there had been a marriage in the offing. Hartman had never even intimated at this during the years of their friendship. But still, Dawson *was* going to marry her, and he couldn't have been very happy about the change of plans. His recent history of violence toward women made him an even stronger candidate in Clint's mind. Of course, he had a rich family behind him, which also might have had something to do with Rick Hartman taking the blame all those years ago.

Today he was going to get the real story.

He knew this was ambitious planning for one day, but he was tired of looking over his shoulder for hired killers.

It was bad enough that he already had to be wary of would-be legends.

It stopped today.

As he got out of the cab, he abandoned any idea of waiting in a doorway to follow Morgan somewhere quiet. The man's office was quiet enough.

He went up and presented himself to Miss Annie Bennett.

"How nice to see you back so soon, Mr. Adams," she said. "Can I help you?"

"I need to see Mr. Morgan again, Annie."

"Um . . ." she looked nervous.

"Let me guess," he said. "He told you not to let me in to see him anymore."

"Why, yes," she said, "how did you know that?"

"A lucky guess. Annie," he said, leaning on her desk, "I think this would be a good time for you to go and check your petticoats."

"I'm not wearing—"

"Just take a break," he said.

"Why?"

"Because I'm going back to Mr. Morgan's office. Now, if I do it while you're here, you're liable to lose your job. However, if I do it while your desk is empty. . . ."

"There's no way I can stop you?" she asked.

"None."

She smiled and stood up.

"I think I'll go out and sneak a cigarette," she said. "They don't like smoking in here."

"What's the world coming to when you can't smoke in the workplace?" he asked.

She smiled again and hurried from the office. Clint took the hallway to James Morgan's office and entered without knocking.

"Annie, I said—" Morgan started, but he stopped when he looked up from his desk and saw Clint. "Adams. I don't underst—"

"Henry Enright," Clint said.

"What?"

"He's one of yours."

"Oh, that man you were asking about. I told you I don't know—"

"He's a Pinkerton, Morgan. You know that."

"Not anymore."

"Then you did lie to me about knowing him?"

Morgan averted his eyes and said, "Yes."

"Why?"

"Because he's a disgrace."

"Because he was working for himself?"

"Yes."

"I need to find him."

"We can't have a scandal—"

"I'll try to save your job, Morgan," Clint said, "but I need Enright."

"Why? What did—"

"He put the price on my head for somebody. I want to know who."

"Bloody stupid . . ." Morgan shook his head.

"Where is he?"

Morgan didn't speak.

"If he's a disgrace, why are you—oh, I think I get it," Clint said, as he flashed on something. "You brought him into the Pinkertons, didn't you? And if they find out what he was doing, it would look bad for you."

Morgan stiffened, lifting his chin.

"You'd end up back in the field—or worse, fired."

Still nothing.

"Maybe I should have a talk with William about you," Clint said.

"He wouldn't listen to you."

Clint smiled and said, "We'll see, James. We'll see."

He'd only taken two steps before Morgan called, "Wait!"

FORTY

According to Morgan, Henry Enright had fallen on hard times of late, and was staying at a cheap hotel on the Barbary Coast. When Clint got there, he was pleased to find that the hotel was a safe enough distance away from The Bucket of Blood saloon that Enright may not have heard about the slight ruckus there.

When Clint entered the hotel, the clerk behind the desk seemed to be dozing, but there were enough flies buzzing around him to indicate that he might have been dead. When Clint got closer, he could smell the whiskey and knew there'd be no waking this fellow up today. He looked for the register and found that the clerk was sleeping on it. He slipped the man's "pillow" from beneath his head without disturbing his slumber and leafed through it. He had to go back through a few weeks of nearly empty pages before he found the entry that said H. Enright was in Room 6.

Clint felt sure that Morgan still knew more than he was telling, but knowing where Enright was staying was enough for him to let the rest go. He figured Morgan knew what Enright was doing, and that the hard times Enright had fallen on were probably a result of the fact that Clint was still alive.

And he intended to stay that way.

As he eased his way down the hall toward Room 6, he drew his gun. The Barbary Coast was no place to get careless, not even in a flophouse like this one.

When he reached Room 6, he pressed his ear to the door and heard nothing. He was about to kick it in when the door across the hall opened and an old woman appeared. She didn't look surprised to see him.

"He ain't in there, so there's no use in ruining the door," she said.

"Do you know where he is?"

She nodded, but said nothing. He took some coins out of his pocket and gave them to her. He wasn't even sure how much was there, but it satisfied her.

"Room thirteen, at the end of the hall," the woman said. "There's a girl there only charges a dollar or two for her company."

"Thanks."

She nodded, closed her door, went up the hall ahead of him, and down the stairs. He continued on to Room 13 and pressed his ear to that door. This time he heard something. The squeaking of bedsprings, and somebody moaning and grunting. He tried the doorknob before kicking it in, but it turned easily and the door opened.

The man on the soiled bed was too busy to notice that Clint had entered the room. He had the girl's skinny legs hanging over his arms, so that her butt was in the air while he pounded into her. She turned her head at that moment and saw Clint, and there was a bored look on her face, which was wasted. She could have been twenty, or fifty.

"You'll have to come back later, honey," she said, "I'm a little busy right now."

"Sorry to interrupt," Clint said, "but I have to talk to Mr. Enright, there."

"Huh? What?" the man said. He looked at Clint, his eyes vacant, his face sweaty, his hair wet and lank. Apparently, they had been going at it for some time. The scent of sex was thick in the air, but also the smell of sweaty, dirty bodies.

"Are you Enright?"

The man frowned.

"Who wants to know?"

Clint held his gun up so Enright could see it.

"I'm Enright."

"Let's go to your room and talk."

"I paid this bitch two dollars," Enright said.

"I'll pay you back."

"Plus five?"

"Plus two," Clint said. "Double your money."

Enright dropped the girl's legs and withdrew from her. His long, skinny dick bobbed in the air until he grabbed his clothes from the floor and held them over his crotch.

"Let's go."

"Don't you want to get dressed first?"

"Nobody's gonna care," Enright said, and went out into the hall.

The girl rolled over onto her belly and eyed Clint, her legs in the air behind her.

"Why don't you come back when your business is finished."

"I don't think I'll have any money left," he said, "but thanks."

He closed the door and followed Enright's skinny ass down to Room 6.

When he got there, Enright was sitting on the bed, holding his pants in his lap. His shirt and shoes were on the floor.

"Money first," he said, "then we talk."

Clint took out four dollars and gave it to him. It was the easy way. He'd save the hard way for later.

"Whataya want? You want to hire me? I don't come cheap."

"I can see that," Clint said.

"This place?" Enright said. "This is the result of a temporary setback."

Enright looked to be in his early forties, very skinny with long, thin hair parted in the middle, and a sparse excuse for a mustache on his almost missing upper lip. He had a weak chin and watery eyes. He did not look like a Pinkerton operative.

"I don't want to hire you."

"Then what do you want?"

"I want to ask you some questions."

"About what?"

"About a lawyer named Robert Barkley."

Enright screwed his face up as if he'd bitten into a lemon.

"Did Barkley send you here?"

"Not exactly," Clint said. "I got your name from James Morgan."

"Morgan," Enright said. "He referred you?"

"This is not exactly a referral."

"Look, mister," Enright said, reaching beneath his wadded-up pants to scratch his crotch, "I was busy when you got here and I'm lookin' to go back to what I was doing. Who are you and what do you want?"

"My name is Clint Adams," he answered, "and I want to know who hired you and put a price on my head."

At that moment, Enright fired a shot from the gun he'd been holding under his pants.

FORTY-ONE

The muzzle flash set the pants afire and Enright tossed them away convulsively. He'd hurried the shot so much that he missed, but the bullet passed so close to Clint's ear that it enraged him.

He stepped forward and pistol-whipped the ex-Pinkerton before he could get off another shot. As the man slumped to the floor, bleeding from a scalp wound, the little .32-caliber pistol he'd been holding fell from his hand. Clint picked it up and wondered if the wadded-up, heavy tweed pants the man had fired through had deflected the small bullet enough to save his life. That thought enraged him some more, and he angrily kicked the unconscious man in the ribs.

Jesus, he'd almost been killed by a wasted wretch in a flophouse on the Barbary Coast with the smell of sex and dirty, unwashed bodies still in his nostrils. He walked to the window, opened it, then slammed the door shut. He walked to the smoldering pants and stomped on them, then sat down to wait for the man to regain consciousness.

The shot had attracted no attention.

Enright moaned, announcing that he was coming to. When he opened his eyes, he saw the barrel of Clint's gun just off the tip of his nose.

"I'm in a bad mood, Enright," Clint said, "so you better answer this question right the first time. Who hired you to go to Barkley and buy my death?"

Enright couldn't take his eyes off the barrel of the gun, and didn't seem to notice the blood that was trickling down the bridge of his nose and dripping off the end of it.

"Dawson."

Clint wasn't sure he'd heard right.

"What?"

"The man's name is Dawson."

"Wesley Dawson?"

Enright shook his head and blood splattered. For the first time he became aware of it. He touched his face and looked at the redness on his fingertips.

"I'm bleeding."

"Yes, you are."

"Am I shot?"

"No," Clint said, and added, "not yet. If it's not Wesley Dawson, then who is it?"

"The father," Enright said, "the old man. Eric Dawson. He's got all the money."

"And he sent you to Barkley?"

"That's right."

"Specifically to put a price on my head?"

"Yeah."

"Did he say why?"

"I never asked," Enright said. "He paid me a lot of money."

"It didn't last very long, did it?" Clint said.

Enright made a face. "I thought there'd be more coming."

"Your kind always do," Clint commented.

"Whataya gonna do?" Enright asked. "You're not g-gonna kill me, are you?"

"Why not?" Clint asked. "You just tried to kill me."

"I was defending myself," the man said. "I thought you were gonna kill me."

"If I wanted to kill you," Clint said, "you'd be dead. How do I get to Dawson?"

"I don't know."

"Can you get to him?"

"No," Enright said. "He won't have nothing to do with me."

"He's blaming you because I'm still alive?"

"I guess."

"Why not blame Barkley?" Clint asked. "He's the one who hired the men."

"I don't know," Enright said. "Ask him."

Clint didn't know if by "him" Enright meant Barkley or Dawson, but either one was a good idea.

"Can I get up?" Enright said. "I got to wash my face."

Clint stood up and said, "Wash the rest of yourself, too, while you're at it. You stink."

Enright staggered to his feet.

"You ain't gonna kill me?"

"Yes, I am," Clint said, and the man's eyes went wide. "If I ever see you again, I won't even say a word. I'll just kill you."

"You won't see me," Enright assured him, "ever again."

"You better hope not," Clint said, and left.

FORTY-TWO

Clint managed to get a message to Chyna Delaney only because everyone in San Francisco knew where her family lived. He waited at his hotel, hoping she would get the message and act instantly, and was gratified to see that she had, and did. When she came walking in he approached her almost too eagerly, so that she got the wrong idea.

"Your message said it was important," she said as he took her arm. "I thought we agreed that last night—"

"This isn't about last night," he said. "It's about ten years ago."

"What?"

"I want to talk to your fiancé," he said. "Can you arrange it?"

"Wesley?"

"And his father, Eric."

"His father?" she asked, and then started shaking her head. "I might be able to get you together with Wesley, but not his father."

"How about your father?" he asked. "Can he get me in to Eric Dawson?"

"What is this about?"

"I told you," Clint said. "It's about the murder of your sister ten years ago."

173

"By Rick Hartman."

"No," Clint said, "not by Rick Hartman."

"How can you say—wait a minute. You do know him?"

"Yes, I do," Clint said. "He's probably one of the best friends I have."

"God*damn* you, Clint—"

"Look, Chyna," he interrupted, "Rick didn't kill your sister, and I can prove it."

"How?"

"I have to talk to Wesley and his father."

"Why his father?"

"Because," Clint explained, "Eric Dawson put a price on my head. He's been trying to have me killed for months."

"That's crazy," she said. "Why would he do that?"

Clint looked around, looking for a private place to talk. He finally just pulled her aside to one of the sofas in the lobby.

"It's taken me a while to put this together," he said, "but the attempts on my life are connected with the murder of your sister."

She looked dazed.

"How can that be?"

"First, tell me if there's something big coming up for the Dawson family."

"Well, there's the wedding—"

"Something bigger."

"—and the election."

"What election?"

"Eric Dawson is running for governor."

"Endorsed by your father?"

"Well, yes, but—"

"And any hint of scandal could ruin his chances to be governor."

"So?"

"So what possible scandal could there be?"

"There isn't any," she said. "Mr. Dawson is clean. That's why my father is endorsing him."

"But is his son clean?" Clint asked.

"Wesley?" She shook her head. "He's a little wild—"

"He beats women."

"Where did you hear that?"

"Is it true?"

She hesitated, then said, "His temper does get the better of him on occasion."

"Why would you marry a man like that?"

"Clint," she said, "I married a man for love when I was young, and he broke my heart."

"So this time you're marrying for the sake of the family?"

"Yes."

"What if I told you that the man you're going to marry killed your sister."

She stared at him.

"You don't have any proof."

"As much as you have that Rick Hartman did it," he said. "Maybe more."

"Like what?"

"Like he was angry that your sister dumped him. Like his past history of violence toward women. Has he ever hit you?"

"My father would have him killed if he did."

"I need to talk to him, Chyna," Clint said. "He's the only other logical suspect."

"But what does this have to do with someone trying to kill you?"

"I'm not sure," he said. "I only know that Eric Dawson has a price on my head, and it can't be a coincidence. There's some connection, and I need to talk to them to find out what it is."

She paused, thinking over what he was saying to her.

"If there's any chance that Wesley killed your sister," he said softly, "you don't want to marry him."

"All right," she said, "all right. I'll get you a meeting with Wesley. I don't know what I can do about his father."

"That'll be a start," he said.

"Tell me when," she said.

He did, and then he said, "And you tell me where."

She did.

FORTY-THREE

Clint found the meeting place odd. Chyna told him that her family owned a building in Chinatown, which was empty at the moment.

"How will you get Wesley there?" he asked.

"I'll tell him that this meeting is important to both our families," she said. "If he thinks that something is important to his father, he'll do it."

She gave Clint a key to the building, which she said was a warehouse with some offices upstairs.

"Meet us inside."

"Whoa," he said, "why are you coming?"

"Because," she said, "this meeting *is* important to both our families."

"Well," he said, "then I have a suggestion . . ."

Clint found the warehouse with no problem and let himself in. He got there early, just in case Chyna had decided to double-cross him. The way things were going he wasn't sure who to trust.

The building had two stories: the main storage area and upstairs offices. He checked both levels and found them abandoned except for some empty crates and barrels on the warehouse floor. He sat on one of the barrels to await the arrival of Wesley Dawson.

Clint had found two lamps when he arrived, and now there was a pool of light in the center of the warehouse floor. Clint sat on a barrel just beyond that circle. When Wesley Dawson finally arrived and entered, he could not see Clint immediately.

"Chyna?" he called. "Hello?" He stepped into the light. He looked to be in his early to mid-thirties.

"She's not here, Wesley."

Dawson squinted and tried to look into the darkness.

"Who's that?"

Clint got up from the barrel and came into the light.

"I'm the man your father's been trying to have killed for the last two months."

"What? What the hell are you talking about? What have you done with Chyna?"

"Chyna's fine, Wesley," Clint said. "She arranged this little meeting for us."

"Why?"

"Because I have some questions."

"I don't have to answer your questions," Dawson said.

"You don't, but you will."

"Oh? Why will I?"

"Because if you don't I'll bring Rick Hartman back here to San Francisco to talk to the police."

"Hart—he'd be arrested as soon as he got here."

"Maybe," Clint said, "but he'd do a lot of talking, the kind that might damage your daddy's campaign."

Dawson thought about that for a few moments, then said grudgingly, "What do you want to know?"

"I want to know what happened that night."

"What night?"

"The night Carmen Sternwood was killed."

"Hartman—"

"No," Clint said. "See, I know Rick Hartman didn't kill her, so that just leaves you."

Wesley Dawson did not respond.

"You were angry that she dumped you for Rick Hartman, but then he left. What happened then?"

No answer.

"Come on, Wesley," Clint prodded. "If you have any kind of conscience, this has been eating you up inside all these years. It's time to get it out. It's just you and me."

Finally, Wesley crumbled and started to talk. It was even easier than Clint had anticipated.

"I didn't mean to."

"Didn't mean to do what?"

"To kill her," he said.

"What happened?"

"It's like you said," he answered. "She dumped me for him, and then he left. He never intended to marry her. I found her at his hotel, in his room after he left. I told her I still loved her and would marry her, but she laughed. She laughed at me! Said I wasn't half the man he was."

Dawson seemed to be looking inside himself at the scene from his past.

"What happened then?"

"I don't know," he said. "Next thing I knew she was on the floor. I ran."

"And told your father?"

"Yes."

"And he fixed it up for you?"

"That's right," Dawson said. "He fixed it to look like Hartman did it."

"Wesley," Clint said, "it's time to talk to the law."

"I'm afraid Wesley won't be doing that, Mr. Adams," a voice said from the darkness behind him.

Clint turned and saw two men with guns step out of the darkness. There must have been a door he didn't know about, and James Morgan and Henry Enright had come through it.

"Well, well, Mr. Morgan," Clint said. "What brings you out into the field?"

"Money, and lots of it," Morgan said. "Enright, get Wesley out of here."

"And then what, Morgan? You going to kill me yourself? Collect the bounty on my head?"

"Killing for money's not so hard," Morgan said. "After you've done it once—" He stopped short, as if he realized he'd overstepped himself. "Henry, get him out."

"Now I get it," Clint said. "Dawson sent you to clean up the mess, only she wasn't dead yet."

"What?" Wesley Dawson said. "You know, when I left I thought she was alive, but later my father told me she was dead."

"She was," Morgan said, "after I left." He looked at Clint. "Old Man Dawson told me to fix it, so I did."

"You killed her?" Wesley yelled. "But I loved her!"

"She wasn't a proper wife for you, Wesley," Morgan said. "Not after she took up with that gambler." He looked at Clint again. "At least, that's what his old man said." He addressed himself to Enright again. "Get Wesley out of here. I'll take care of Adams."

Enright crossed the room to Wesley and grabbed his arm. "No!" Wesley shouted, and grabbed Enright's arm, causing his gun to go off. Wesley grunted and fell to the ground.

The shot gave Clint the split second he needed. Morgan took his eye off him for just that long, and Clint drew and fired. The bullet struck Morgan in the chest, making his eyes bug out in shock and surprise.

Clint turned to see Enright standing over the fallen Wesley.

"No, don't—" Enright shouted, but it was too late. There was a shot from above and Enright fell to the ground next to the writhing Wesley Dawson.

Clint checked Morgan to make sure he was dead, then walked to Enright. By that time Chyna had come down from the second level with her brother, Charles, who was holding a gun.

"We heard it all, Clint," she said. "Hartman didn't do it."

"No, he didn't."

Charles stared down at Enright, his gun held lightly in his hand.

"Is he dead?" he asked. "I never shot anyone before."

Clint took the gun from his limp hand and said, "Let's hope you never have to again."

FORTY-FOUR

"It's all over," General Sternwood said. "Eric Dawson's march to the governor's mansion is finished."

"How's Wesley?" Clint asked.

"He'll live," Sternwood said, "to talk to the police some more."

They were alone in Sternwood's study. The old man had a blanket over his legs and looked even older and more tired than before.

"Your friend is free of any blame."

"I don't think he ever knew he was being blamed," Clint said. "I'll see if I can keep it that way. I'm still puzzled abut one thing, though."

"What's that?"

"Why me?" Clint asked. "Why would Eric Dawson want me killed?"

"Apparently, by the time I hired the Pinkertons, James Morgan was in a position to make sure I never found Rick Hartman. Dawson knew where he was, of course, but was content to leave him be, as long as he didn't come back to San Francisco."

"Which he never did, but not because he was afraid," Clint said. "He just found a place he liked and has stayed here all these years."

"Well, Dawson was happy with that, until he got th
opportunity to run for governor. Then he couldn't afford t
leave Hartman out there."

"But why come after me?"

"You were Hartman's great friend. If he killed Hartma
you would not let it rest."

"I get it," Clint said, the light finally dawning. "Onc
he got rid of me, he could have Rick killed."

"Only killing you turned out to be not so easy."

"It's ironic."

"What is?"

"It was his putting a bounty on my head that ultimatel
brought me here."

"And brought about his demise."

"But all he loses is the governor's mansion?" Clin
asked. "Can the police touch him?"

"Don't worry about that, Mr. Adams," Sternwood said
"He will not get away with what he did, either to you o
to me and my family. It's a shame, though."

"What is?"

"In spite of everything," Sternwood said, "I thought h
would make a great governor of California. Now we'
never know."

Somehow, Clint didn't find that much of a shame.

Watch for

STRANGLER'S VENDETTA

213th novel in the exciting GUNSMITH series
from Jove

Coming in October!

J. R. ROBERTS
THE GUNSMITH

LONGARM

**Explore the exciting Old West with one
of the men who made it wild!**